SexMagick 2

Men Conjuring Erotic Fantasy

edited by
Cecilia Tan

With Our Compliments

Thanks for being a supporter of erotic literature and the erotic imagination! Please enjoy this book. If you would like to see more like it, please visit www.circlet.com and use promo code 2014love to receive 20% off any ebook or mail order.

Circlet Press, Inc.
Cambridge, MA

Circlet Press, Inc.
1770 Massachusetts Avenue, #278
Cambridge, MA 02140
http://www.circlet.com/circlet/home.html
circlet-info@circlet.com

Copyright © 1997 by Circlet Press, Inc.
Cover photograph copyright © 1995 by Robert Rausch.
All rights reserved.

Typeset and printed in the United States of America.

ISBN 1-885865-09-0

Individual copyrights to the works represented in this volume are held by the respective authors and artists of the works.

This text cannot be distributed, reproduced, transcribed, photocopied, uploaded, downloaded, or otherwise transformed into similar or any other media without express written consent of the publisher and authors.

Circlet Press titles are distributed to bookstores in the U.S.A. and Canada by the LPC Group, (800) 626-4330.

Circlet Press titles are distributed in the U.K. and Europe by Turnaround Ltd., London.

For a catalog or more information about our complete line of erotic science fiction and fantasy titles, contact Circlet Press directly at our address above.

SexMagick 2

Contents

Introduction

This is the second volume of stories I have edited for Circlet Press on the theme of SexMagick. Volume One, a collection of women authors and female-centered erotic power, spoke of personal transformations and liberation. Volume Two, on the other hand, presents the work of mostly male authors, and the stories focus on masculine erotic power.

We have herein incarnations of phallocentric ancient Gods, the unique uses of the sexual talents of certain male exorcists and conjurers, and homoerotic fantasies where gay men bring life to dying worlds. But beyond the obvious maleness of these stories, there is something more, as you will find these are all stories in which strong bonds between the participants are formed. Unlike the women's stories, which left individuals alone at the end of the erotic magic, prepared to meet what challenges might come next, the men here lean toward the formation of everlasting pairs, the reuniting of old lovers, and in one case the permanent spiritual and romantic bonding of a trio. Even the one story that goes against the grain of commitment, "Fleeing Gods," I include as a humorous parting shot at the stereotypes themselves, with Zeus himself playing the part of the lusty sexist. I did not set out seeking such a theme specifically, but it has been wonderful to see the collection come together in that way of its own accord ... as if by magic.

If I had to give a rational explanation, it would be a fairly simple one: the stereotypes about men, and about men's sexual writing (commonly referred to as pornography) are untrue. The common doctrine about men's sexual attitudes is, of course, that they are unconcerned with love and romance and only want the physical satisfaction, and that therefore men's sexual writing dehumanizes women, making them lust objects and nothing more, etc. etc. You can find long-winded arguments to this effect elsewhere. Yes, there is a huge porn industry built on low-quality mass-produced films, magazines, and yes, stories, and in such material one can find heaps of evidence to support the stereotypes and the accusations about the evils of pornography. But that was not what I found in my submission pile, not at all.

What I see here are the erotic fantasies of intelligent, honest men, who are not afraid to admit that everlasting love is a part of their sexual fantasies. I see that commitments sealed by blood, magic, and with the power of Gods are central to their most wild and deep imaginings of sex. And I am proud to bring them into your hands.

Cecilia Tan
February 1997

The Night of Pan

Kenneth Deigh

The sun is hot and bright above the dry grass and sea of tents. I feel parched and worn, bleached by the harsh, dry light of this unseasonable warm spring day. I am standing on a small ridge, overlooking the flat bottom of a narrow valley, with green, tree- drenched slopes rising to either side. Every square foot of hard, flat ground has been claimed by merchants, performers, priestesses, priests, or the members of the wandering tribes that have gathered here for their annual rites, welcoming the return of Spring.

I have felt different this year: alone and separate from family and clan. It hasn't felt like this since my first gathering, and I feel a numb sense of loss. I go through the motions. I share the cup in circle. I dance the fire. I take my turn at the drums. But my heart is not here. Neither is it anywhere.

Five years ago, I had shared these things with Amira. Together we danced the flames of the bonfire, lifted the cup to the powers of Earth and Sky, and spilled ourselves into the loving embrace of Goddess and God. She was my equal in every way, calling the best from me at every turn, lioness to my lion. And she is with me no more.

I have never been good at letting go of anything I wanted to keep, and so it was when Amira left. I held on to her in my heart. At first I joined the dance with other women, used their love to wash away the first pain, to quiet to heat of my loss. But no one else could call up my passion as she had, and so I withdrew, until now, as I say, I merely go through the motions.

I have become an outsider. How can I do my work as Priest, when I no longer feel the God within me? When I no longer sense the caress of the Goddess in every embrace? I have no answers.

After a last long look at the milling faces of my chosen family and our extended tribe, I turn from the festival site and walk up the slope and into the trees. I take nothing with me.

I know that there is nothing but wilderness for many days on foot in the direction I have chosen, and after the first few hours I lose myself in a trance of walking. The forest surrounds me, touches me gently with sound. I know that it wants to heal me, but I cannot feel it in my heart. I walk on, beyond time, beyond memory, into a twilight beyond any state of consciousness I have yet encountered ... and still I walk on.

Slowly I become aware that I am being drawn forward. As I surrender to the summons, all fatigue falls away from my muscles, and fire begins to rise through my bones. I am trotting now. My body dances like rising in the night. My mouth stretches into a wide grin. A wild ecstasy flows through my veins, ignites my soul, and raises me out of myself. I leap forward! The drums rise about me, calling to the deepest part of me by name! "Pan!" they cry, "Come to us!"

From shadowed depths of tides unborn
I call you forth to light unknown

Ride to me in lust's disguise
Io Pan, Io Pan
seduce my reason inflame my sight

The voices reach me now, twining with the drums in their now-irresistible evocation of my presence. Old memories arise; images from before mankind flash before me. I am the Old One, the goat-footed God of the primordial forest. I romp through the darkness, still far beyond the circle of light cast by the fires of that woodland temple, where even now I know the Priestesses summon me. Dancing here in the dark, I listen to them sing to me, call to me, and to my power. I remember this song. I remember the dance. The men ride their sacred drums at the edge of the circle The voices of the drums sing a deep primal rhythm that rises in me as an overpowering lust. The curving horns above my brow glisten with a velvety sheen of sweat, and my musk excites even the stones beneath my hooves.

This lust transforms me. I feel the call writhing within me, from the depths of my body, hardening and drawing me here, into the light before the Temple of great ancient trees. I pause, finally resisting the pull of her voice, that mysteriously familiar voice that calls to me above all the others. I watch as lightly clad priestesses fling themselves around the wheel of the year in their dance of desire. I can feel the lust they raise within themselves. It mounts, and draws me out, draws me to them.

It is Walpurgisnacht, the night for dancing widdershins about the foundations of the world. These dancing pagans have called me up to their fire, to their song, and they do not know what they have called. Only she knows, the High Priestess, swaying before the altar, piled high with grapes and pinecones, with a full cup of new wine. She remembers the old song that calls me forth, that summons my own peculiar madness.

> *Shake me from my waking slumber*
> *horned one, god's own son*
> *come renew my heart's desire*
> *passion of man, lo Pan*
> *lo Pan, Pan!*

It is an old song, sung in different words, in diverse tongues, yet ever the same and thrilling call. I am just outside the light, and I feel the call so strongly now, so deep within me. I feel it in a place that has never been silent of desire, but ever wanting, ever thirsting after life, and more.

In a final rush I leap the fires and land snarling in the midst of the circle. For a moment the shock of my appearance breaks the spell, and the song falters. I could escape now, if I desired escape. Then the High Priestess turns to me, and sings from the depths, merging with the pounding drums and the whirring feet.

I want them to run from me in terror, but now they are drugged by the same spell that has drawn me here, and they leave their dance and their drums and gather about me. I strike out, enraged. I lift one large and hairy man high above my head, feeling his weight shift as he squirms in my grasp, and throw him to the ground, and still the song burns deeper and hotter within me.

> *Wild half-man, rutting goat*
> *from fire born and lust begotten*
> *rise upon your pounding bone*
> *writhing serpent of life yet born*

I move through them like a wave through water and find myself before the high Priestess. Here I pause, stepping outside of time to take in her heat, her beauty, and the heady power she holds in drawing me here. I look into her eyes and see Her, She with whom I have danced this dance through eternity. She looks up at me, takes my face gently in her hands, and says, in a soft voice that cuts through the spell she weaves, "I have never forsaken you, my Beloved." She smiles, throws back Her head, and laughs wildly, drawing me to Her. Clasping me to Her with a power that equals my own, She bares Her firm breasts to my hunger. My tongue discovers an erect nipple and I suck the fluid ecstasy of Her arousal. She reaches down and grasps my burning shaft. The song begins anew around us as passion leaps like the flames.

> *Goat-footed wandering god of the wood*
> *O Pan! Io Pan!*
> *break through the shelter of reason and right*
> *Io Pan! Io Pan Pan! Pan Pan!*

The wave of primal lust rages through me and I throw her to the ground, inflamed by desire. I tear her clothes from her, and she opens herself to me, like the womb of the All Mother. I bury myself within her to the rhythm of the rekindled drum song. My flesh enters her warm and welcoming body; she takes the violent rage of Life and balances it with Form. And still she sings inside my head, though her outer voice is now consumed in passion.

> *I have arisen from spiraled stone*
> *torn from life and spurned by man*
> *still I burn with life's desire*
> *all to create! all to devour!*
> *I spill my seed upon the stone*
> *returning to life what life has torn*
> *I am Pan! Io Pan! Io Pan Pan!*
> *Pan! Io Pan!*

I am lost in the thrusting exaltation of my desire. No longer confined to this vessel, having given the gift of my seed, I feel myself growing, spilling out of this form into spirit. Like a flame in a field of dry grass, I rush through these people, filling them with my power. I am the dawn! I am the star of the morning unchained! I feel myself rising once more to the peak, becoming lost in the rites of desire. I am becoming the words, becoming the song, becoming the seed!

With a last cry of ecstasy I send the spark of my life through the body of my lover, and into the Earth, where She welcomes me. As the light begins to fade, and my body begins to cool and stiffen, I hear the worshippers as they gather about that still form, lifting what was me above their heads in silence, and carrying me out between the fires of the gate, and back into the womb of the earth.

I awaken. The sun is warm and friendly, caressing my bare skin with a gentle stirring. I feel strangely whole, rested and complete. I feel her warmth along my back, and I turn gently, so as not to awaken my priestess. She smiles as I draw her into my arms. With a full heart I look over the sea of tents, knowing that I have come Home.

The Magic of Sexual Beings

Robert Knippenberg

Let me tell you right up front that I do not believe in magic, UFOs, ghosts, or God. I'm skeptical, as only a "recovering Catholic" can be, and I like to deal with real things, things I can touch and feel. On the other hand, I am smart enough to know that there *are* lots things we don't as yet understand—things about the universe, and life and ourselves, and that these things sometimes appear to be magical or mystical because of our ignorance or lack of experience.

I also know, because of the stupid way most of us have been raised, that all of us have a deep-seated desire to believe. It starts when you're an infant, when things just happen, and there are no explanations because words are just another wonderful stimulus coming out of nowhere and stirring you because all you are is a wriggling bunch of nerve cells greedy to experience everything.

15

And then later, before you have even heard of cause and effect, you're exposed to fairy tales, things like "Cinderella" and "When you wish upon a star..." and religion, Christ up there nailed to his cross with his fake blood, so beautiful, sad and naked—God what an awful thing to do to little kids, and especially to little girls!

And then it just continues as you're growing up. It's like there's this whole underground movement of the irrational, a plot to make you think things are different from what they are.

For example, how many of you men out there have looked at a woman's magazine lately? Forget about all the lame advice on health and sex and relationships and diet, and just look at the ads. Is that reality? No wonder most of us women are so screwed up.

Anyway, before I get off on that topic, the point is that most of us, men and women both, are still children inside. All of us have dreams and all of us want to believe in magic. If we didn't we would never buy any of the crap they advertise. I don't mean this to be a lecture on the stupidity of American society, but you may as well know it's one of my favorite topics, and it will inevitably creep in now and then.

I'm telling you all this so you'll understand what happened.

It started with June asking me to go to the circus with her. Whenever I think about circuses and fairs and carnivals my initial reaction is one of disgust. I hate the phoniness, the garishness, and the obvious clumsy greediness of them. They're all cons, and all the games are rigged, and the food is unhealthy and unsanitary, and the women and men who perform are really old and/or ugly behind their makeup and elaborate costumes. Worst of all I know that the people who run these things have this superior insider attitude and are laughing at all us suckers who come there to get bilked out of their money.

But that's just my rational side, and Junie knows it. She kept insisting, knowing that once I got there the bright lights and the noise and the milling crowds and the glitter and the smells and the rides would take over, and then the kid in me would pop out and just have a great time.

The reason Junie knows me so well is that we have been best friends for as long as I can remember. We grew up together and do a lot of things together. We even discovered sex together, first with each other, and then with boys, and we're still lovers occasionally.

It's always struck me as odd that women seem to be able to be closer friends then men. Maybe it's a homophobic thing, but men friends don't touch each other very much, while women do. It's probably got something to do with competition. Men are always trying to "win," even in simple things like conversations. It's like we're all still living in the trees and they're stuck on figuring out who is going to lead the troupe. Women, even in their conversations, are much more concerned with keeping the troupe together. So even when we're very different from each other, we're basically concerned with our agreements rather than our differences.

That is not to say that we don't compete with each other. In fact, women can be much more vicious then men. Men play the game all the time and seem to have established some rules—with us there are no rules. We don't want to just win, we want to destroy our opponents, even if it means destroying ourselves. If you think about it, about what we are and where we came from, this makes sense.

Imagine us as we once were, hairy shambling creatures on the plains of Ethiopia. The male Australopithecus wants to be the leader, but he can't kill all his rival males because he needs them to be followers and to help him when danger threatens. But the female is competing to be a breeder. She doesn't need her rivals to be alive. In fact, given the short attention span of

17

the males, the only way she can be sure that it will be her genes which will be passed on is to obliterate her competition.

Well, anyway, maybe that explains a little bit why I did what I did to Martha, and why June and I are so close. All three of us are different from each other, and yet we all have our similarities. Junie and I are so physically unalike we have never been in competition when it comes to men.

Junie is little and round and blonde and sweet, while I am the tall and statuesque type, and my hair is long and absolutely black. We've never attracted the same kinds of guys and have never wanted the kind of guy that the other attracts. Maybe it was all the times we've made love, or maybe it's the notes we used to pass in school, but we have always had this ability to communicate with each other on some other wavelength. I still don't know what it was that happened between me and Martha, but then that's what this is all about, and it will get really confusing if I start jumping ahead, so that's why I have to tell you about it from the beginning.

Junie and I went to the circus, and we were having a great time, as we always do together. And even though I said "no," and was giving her one of my usual spiels about not believing in all that crap, and how destructive it was to think there was anything to it, I went with her to the fortune-teller's tent. She loves this stuff and is always reading her horoscope (she's a Libra and I'm a Scorpio) and reading mine to me.

She insisted I go in first, and we were both giggling like a couple of kids as she pushed me through the curtained door-way over which hung a little glowing sign that said "Madame Tantru."

Inside it was, as I expected, hung with the usual dark cheap drapes, and dimly lit with colored lights and candles. And the Madame herself, sitting at her little round table, was suitably dressed in a robe covered with mystical symbols like some nun gone mad. She had a nice smile though, and was pretty and not too old either. I'd guess in her mid-thirties maybe.

"Margaret," she repeated, after I had told her my name, and the way she said it made me stop feeling silly and superior all of a sudden. She was staring at my hand, which she was holding gently but firmly in both of hers.

"It is a good name for you. It may have been one of your names in a previous existence," she said a moment later.

"I don't believe in reincarnation."

"What we believe doesn't matter. It is what the soul within us has come here to learn that matters. If you are in tune with it, your life will be harmonious. If you are not, if you fight it, you will be unhappy all the time and not know why. It can even make you ill."

The woman had one of those Slavic accents that was probably genuine, but also sounded as if she were emphasizing it to add to her authenticity. I had taken some Russian in college (before I met Henry and dropped out) and recognized the way she put two consonants together in one syllable in a way that is impossible for Romance language speakers to do.

"Am I in tune with my soul?" I asked her. I was still grinning, but her words were starting to get to me, even if I did not realize how much at the time.

"Yes, for the most part. You have a grille on the mount of Venus. This indicates you have a passionate nature. Almost too much so at times. You are a sexual being, Margaret, but I can also see that it suits you."

I couldn't help but blush. As I said, I'm a Scorpio, and even though I am not a believer in astrology, the sign seemed to fit. When I was little I really liked how my fingers felt crossing myself in church, and I swear I can remember masturbating in my crib, so that will give you some idea how important sex is to me. It's where I get my energy from. Most people get sleepy afterwards, but it makes me feel alive and full of zip.

"You are very involved with a man right now, I see. There have been others, but this one is different. He is very different from you, and you are very much in love with him."

"I can't believe you can tell all this just from the lines on my hand," I said. I was still trying to be skeptical, but she was right on target, and what she said sent one of those little shivering chills that only ex-Catholics can feel (I call them the "guilty thrills") up and down my back.

"It's not just the lines. It's shape of your hand and your fingers as well. You have beautiful hands, long slender fingers, and yet strong. There are emanations that come out of our hands. This is why we like to touch things, and each other. You have a great deal of energy, and I can feel from it that there is another. Another woman who is important in your life."

For a moment I thought she meant June. Only a little while earlier, the very hand she was holding had been rubbing June's cunt. We had been riding the Ferris wheel. While we were stopped up on top, I put my hand up the leg of her shorts and we started fooling around with each other. She and her boyfriend Mike had had a little fight and were temporarily not speaking, my Henry was out of town on a real business trip, and we had been "consoling" each other.

I started to giggle, wondering she if was somehow smelling June on my fingers, but then I realized she could be talking about Martha, Henry's wife, and I began to wonder just how much this woman could tell about me. I decided to keep quiet and see.

"This other woman is not like you at all, and yet she is," Madame Tantru continued. "There is a connection between you. A very powerful and dangerous connection."

Then I knew she meant Martha, Henry's wife, a frigid, uptight, churchgoing, silently unhappy bitch. Henry had said that she was different when they first got married, that she was sweet and loving when she was putting him through college.

After he had graduated and gotten his career started, she found out he could never give her the children she wanted, and she changed. Henry had upset her plans for her perfect life, and she could never forgive him for it. She had been making him miserable ever since.

I figured that she had always been a shrew and just started showing it. I could just imagine her using her soft-spoken threats and playing little manipulative games to get what she wanted. Henry is so gentle and self-deprecating that he's easy to make feel guilty. I used to get angry at him sometimes for being so vulnerable, but I also know that's part of the reason I love him. But that's a whole other story in itself, and I'll get to that.

"I've never seen anything quite like it," Madame Tantru said, and she started looking at me then instead of my hand.

"Oh?" was all I said. I couldn't believe she was making something mystical out of simply having an affair with a married man. Not that these things are ever simple, but she must know that a lot of people do them.

"This connection goes back very far. Into the past. It is not just him. It is something deeper than that."

Then was when I started getting uncomfortable. I didn't like the idea of being "connected" to Martha in the present, much less in some supposedly deep way in the past. If I had had my way back then, she would have fallen off the edge of the Earth so I could have Henry all to myself.

She let go of my one hand then, and took the other. "This hand is your potential, what you can be in the future. The other is what you are, what has happened to you already," she said. I remember thinking I'd have to look closely at my hands later to see how much difference there was in the lines.

"Your future could be, well ... you must be careful. There is..." She stopped then. It reminded me of what doctors do sometimes, and it makes your heart sink.

"What?" I blurted out, forgetting my promise to keep quiet. She was good. She had my heart racing.

"Have you ever had any psychic experiences?"

"No. I don't think so." I meant it too. And then I started thinking about how I had met Henry. I wouldn't classify it as a psychic experience, but it certainly wasn't ordinary either. It was like we already knew each other. I had taken a walk down to the marina, and he was getting his sailboat ready by the dock, and we just started talking. Then he asked me if I'd like to go with him, and I remember hearing myself say "yes" before I had even thought about it.

We were only out for an hour or so, but during that time we talked about everything, his job, my going to school, his wife, my latest boyfriend, our attitudes about sex, society and religion and politics. I remember thinking it was the most incredible hour I had ever spent with anyone, and that it only seemed natural for us to go out to dinner the next night, and then afterwards to go to a hotel and make love.

And the whole time in the beginning, neither of us were thinking about the past or the future. We were living totally in the present, in the rapture of each moment, as though nothing else mattered, and it was completely right and honest like nothing else had ever been for either of us.

"I'm surprised," Madame Tantru said. "There are things in your hand I have seen before only very rarely. Look here," and she held her hand open next to mine. "This line indicates power, spiritual power. It is not common at all. Your hand and my hand are similarly marked."

I really couldn't see anything about our hands that struck me. "Does this mean I can read minds like you?" I asked.

"I do not read minds!" she said angrily. "I have been given the ability to help people by telling them about themselves. People's hands reveal them. Anyone can learn to do this."

I tried to apologize then but she interrupted me. "Never mind, it's a common mistake," she said, suddenly calm again. "But you should know better. You have been put here to help others as well."

"Me?" I said.

"I want you to see a friend of mine." She rummaged through a perfectly ordinary purse that she took out from under the table and handed me a little business card. I took it out of politeness. "Promise me you will call him and make an appointment?"

The card looked normal enough. I still have it around somewhere. It said, "Ross Carlton, Advisor," with a phone number but no address. The dramatic way she rolled the three "r's" I almost expected him to appear in a puff of blue smoke.

"You have an unusual palm, Margaret, and Mr. Carlton will be very interested when he sees it. He will know what to do. I will call him and tell him about you."

"OK," I said, suddenly wanting to get out of there and find a ladies' room. It had gotten very weird and I had, of course, no intention of calling the guy. I dropped the card in my purse, and took out my wallet to pay her.

"No, no money. I have not helped you. Please, leave now. And tell your friend outside that she should come back some other time. I am very tired, and will do no more tonight."

And just like that she got up and left through the curtains in the back. I went out and the lighted sign above her doorway went out just as I stepped through.

"Well, what did she say?" said Junie, all excited, of course.

"That she was tired!" I told her. I was laughing, because already it seemed unreal to me, and a real waste of time. "Come on, I got to pee."

23

Well, that's how it started. I would never have called "R-r-ross Car-r-rlton Advisor-r-r," and in fact had forgotten all about him and Madame Tantr-r-ru when things changed.

Henry and I had been together—that is if you call stolen hours being "together"—for about two years at that point. And all that time I had imagined Martha as a kind of cardboard cutout. Whenever Henry talked about her, which was seldom, I pictured her standing, stiffly unmoving, wearing a matronly house dress, hands on her hips, her lips opening and closing like a bad cartoon as her reedy piercing voice berated him.

Henry had shown me a not-very-good picture of her, and she was not an unattractive woman, just ordinary. I guess that's where I got the cardboard from.

And I had never heard her voice. I made that up too. I had never called him at home, even though there were times I wanted to so bad I wanted to scream, or sometimes cry. But I knew it was her when she called me.

I still don't know how she found out about us, but I suppose it was inevitable. Henry is not a good liar. He's too honest. But he can keep his mouth shut and say nothing, so much so sometimes that it still drives me crazy, so I know he didn't tell her. Maybe all the "business trips" were making her suspicious and she was going through his wallet or his things and found my phone number, or one of Henry's little notes. I'll have to remember ask her. I can't believe I haven't, but it doesn't seem important now.

Anyway, Henry may be a brilliant engineer, but he can't remember simple things, and writes down everything on little pieces of paper. I know because I'm always finding them, crumpled up yellow squares that say things like "Pick up car at 2:00" or "Margaret's birthday Tues" or "Get haircut."

Back then I used to keep all of them. I used to paste them in a scrapbook along with the few pictures I had of him, and of the two of us, and the matchbooks, or pieces of the napkins with the names of the hotels we stayed in, and the postcards of places we had been together.

Anyway, her voice was not at all like I thought it would be. The steely hardness and the threat were there, but she also sounded younger and more feminine then I had imagined. "Margaret, I know about you and Henry. I want it to stop! If you don't, you'll be sorry!" she said.

With me, the first thrill of panic is almost like sex. At least until it hits my stomach. Then I get scared and guilty, like a kid caught thinking about doing something bad. Then I get determined. All this happens in less then a second. That time I got angry at the end of it.

"Fuck you! I love him more than you do!" I said, but it was already too late, and I had said it to the dial tone.

Then I sat down, and the thought that I might actually lose Henry made the terror, the guilt, the panic start all over again. I was sure that he would stop seeing me, at least for a while, if she confronted him. Her father owns the consulting firm where Henry works, and even though the old man is semiretired Martha could have gotten him fired. Henry's job means a lot to him, and he would have a tough time getting work somewhere else if Martha's father had put the word out.

I suppose that's why I suddenly decided to call Ross Carlton. I was desperate, and just at that moment I thought of him and it seemed like the only thing to do. I couldn't call June— she's never given me any good advice when it comes to men. She's too much of a romantic, but at the same time she's practical enough to know better than to get involved with married men. I knew she'd start out the conversation with "I told you this would happen..." and that was the last thing I wanted to hear.

I was surprised when Mr. Carlton sounded on the phone like he knew who I was. I hadn't really expected that Madame

Tantru would have called him, and several months had gone by since that night at the circus.

I said that I needed some advice and he seemed to know what I meant even though I didn't explain. He gave me his address and said that I should come over right away, that it was important, that he could sense I was in danger.

I think until he said that, I could have turned back. But suddenly I heard again the threat in Martha's voice, and remembered what Madame Tantru had said, and it was more then than just the thought of losing Henry that made me decide to go.

His brownstone didn't look that different from all the others. It was in an old section of the city, a narrow crowded street that had once been almost a slum, but had been rehabed by the upper middle class moving back in. Amazingly I found a place to park right in front. I think if I had had to drive around to find one, I would have lost my nerve and gone home. It's funny how our lives turn sometimes on stupid little things like that.

I rang the bell, wondering what the hell was I was doing there. I had decided that I would not ring it again, and had just turned to go down the steps when the huge old carved door opened.

This elderly man answered the door looking like a butler from a PBS Playhouse miniseries. He had snow white hair, and was dressed, if not actually in a tuxedo, in a formal-looking black suit and a stiff white shirt with one of those little bow ties. And he was actually wearing white gloves. "I'm looking for Mr. Carlton," I said.

"Call me Ross, Miss Colby. Please come in," he said, his voice formal too, and reassuring.

"So much for the puff of smoke," I remember thinking, following him down the hall, the walls of which were covered lots of mirrors, large and small. It was definitely not your average meeting with someone you don't know for the first time, but since he seemed more like the head butler then anything, it was like everything was under control, and that living here was something he was accomplishing with the utmost efficiency.

We went into his office, and it was just like the rest of the place, all old polished wood, and full of furniture and pictures and lamps out of the 1800s. Somehow you could tell that these weren't just collected antiques; someone had bought it all new, and it had been sitting there ever since. It made me think "How could you not trust a man like this?"

"Please sit down. May I call you Margaret?" he said. He gestured to a chair in front of the huge expanse of gleaming desk he sat behind. I already felt safe, now I felt like I was dealing with a professional.

"Sure," I said, and I began to like him.

He cleared away the inkstand and the few papers on the desk and turned on the brass light with the green glass shade and pulled it closer. "May I see your hands?"

I pulled my chair up closer and leaned over to give him my hands. Somehow it seemed the natural thing to do. He took off his gloves and took mine in both of his, and the way he did it reminded me suddenly of how Henry would stand at the side of the bed and undress before getting in.

His hands were thin and bony and I could see the blue lines of his veins and the age spots on his skin, but they didn't feel hard or dry, and instead his touch was warm and comforting, like he was my grandfather, except that the way he cradled them in both of his was very sensual.

"Very nice," he said, smiling at me. He had incredible eyes, and I felt my face grow warm, as if he meant more than my hands, as if he were holding all of me. Then I felt a tiny tingle between my legs and one of those "guilty thrills" I told you about before, the kind a girl gets when she decides it's time,

27

and stands up and smiles and undresses for a guy for the first time.

"Hey, this is crazy!" I thought, but then I remembered the disapproving scowls of the nuns when they used to look at our hands in school. I had always wanted to pull away and say, "They're my hands!" but this was different—he was lost in the lines, and it would have been rude.

He didn't talk for a long time, and it was like you get sometimes at the beach lying in the sun, kind of warm and hazy, sexy and lazy. You don't know what time it is and you don't care, and when he started asking me questions, I just answered him from far away, and it didn't seem at all strange at the time.

"What is this other woman's name?" he asked.

"Martha."

"Ah. Martha. And she is married to..."

"Henry."

"Yes, Henry. The man you love."

"Yes."

"And how much do you love this Henry?"

"I ... I don't know. A lot, I guess."

"A lot?"

"Yes, a lot."

"Let's be more specific, Margaret. Would you give your life for him if he asked you to?"

"Henry'd never ask me to do a thing like that. He's too..."

"Yes, yes, I know! But if he did. Let's suppose he did."

"I don't know. I guess I would."

"You guess! You had better be sure, my dear. This is not a matter of doing things because you guess!"

Up until that moment I don't think I had ever really tried to put into words how I felt about Henry. I knew I loved him, but we all use that word so much it's hardly descriptive.

We were just happy together, plain and simple, as if it had always been that way and always would be. It didn't even matter what we did—watching TV or a movie, eating or talking or having sex—it was natural and right—like we're the only two people in the world and there is no yesterday or tomorrow.

And the sex had gotten a lot better by then. Henry is not a naturally sexual person like I am. And Martha, when she used to let him do it at all in the beginning, would just lie there like a statue waiting until it was over with, so he was a little shy about it at first. But he was learning, and teaching him had been part of the fun. He had even gotten to the point where he was starting to like some of the kinky stuff. I had been giving him magazines and dirty books to spark his imagination, and he had started coming up with a few things on his own.

And back then, when we were not together, it was like a piece of me was missing, so that I felt like I was just putting in time until the next time I could see him.

It's not that we hadn't talked about the future. We were sure that Martha would never give Henry a divorce. She was too concerned with how it would look, and the scandal it would have caused among her churchy friends and her uptight family. So the plan was that when he had enough money saved to start his own consulting firm we were just going to take off. But we knew it would take a long time, because Martha watched every penny. She still does.

I guess until the moment that Martha called, I hadn't been thinking very realistically about the future. Maybe when you're twenty-five, the future is too vague to worry about.

But at that moment, talking about Henry and Martha with this strange man who didn't feel like a stranger, I realized that the future was real, and that it was a real possibility that Henry would be taken away from me. It made me feel emptier than I had ever felt, and I knew then that I couldn't go on without him.

"I would do anything for him," I said finally, and I meant it so much I felt this little shiver run up my back, and along with it the chilling realization that all kinds of wonderful and terrible possibilities were suddenly possible, and that this man was about to offer them to me.

"Have you ever heard of voodoo, Margaret?"

"Yeah, sure. You make a doll that represents someone you hate. Then you stick pins in it." I was imagining the Martha cutout, small in my hands, and tearing its head off, slowly.

"Yes, that's right, as far as it goes. But the doll really has nothing to do with it. The doll is just a symbol, a way of focusing. You see, Margaret, we are all connected. We are all part of something else. The souls that inhabit each of us temporarily are pieces of that something else. That is why we fall in love with others, because of the connections between our souls."

"I don't see what this has to do with—"

"Some of us have the ability to affect others through that connection. Some of us can reach out and make others feel what we are feeling, experience what we are experiencing. And you are one of those people, Margaret. You have that power. And I can show you how to use it."

"You mean I could do something and somebody else would feel it?"

"Yes."

"But what good is that? How would something like that, even if it were possible, help me with Henry?"

"I understand your skepticism. But just for a moment think about what it would take to make Martha decide to set Henry free."

"I don't know. I can't think of anything that would make her change her mind. She's the kind of woman who gets up at the same time every day, eats at the same time, has all the meals planned out for a week in advance. She goes to church every Sunday, and to choir practice every Thursday. Henry says that she only watches certain things on television, and that the rest of the time the set stays turned off."

"And if that pattern were broken? I don't mean just a little. I mean shattered completely."

"I suppose it would shatter her. It would drive her crazy." The shivering thrill was shooting up and down my spine again, and I could feel it in my head then too, as if my brain had feelings and there were little sparks going off in there. "And where do you think she is most vulnerable? What part of her would be the best place to begin?"

"Her frigidity. She hates sex. Henry told me that she once said that God had invented sex for the purposes of procreation, but the Devil had invented orgasms, and she was proud that she had never had one."

"And if she suddenly started to enjoy sex?"

I pictured her cardboard face getting all scrunched up the way mine does when I come. I've watched myself in mirrors, and I know how I look. But in her case, it would be terror instead of joy!

All this time Mr. Ross Carlton had been holding my hands, and I realized that as we had been having our crazy conversation, his had never been still. His fingers and thumbs had been gliding over mine with small barely noticeable caresses. And while my mind had not really been conscious of it, other parts of me were. Or maybe it was what we were talking about. Or maybe it was something else, something he was doing. Whatever it was, I realized then that the little tingle between my legs had never gone away, and that I was wet down there.

Behind him there was a big old ticking clock with the pendulum swinging, making the silence even deeper.

"Perhaps a demonstration would convince you," he said softly. "What do you suppose that Martha is doing right now?"

31

The clock began striking. It was 8 P.M. "Today's Thursday, so she'd be at choir practice," I said.

Now I felt something else too, a sense of awe, I guess. I was visualizing how it could be done, and thinking of what it might mean if I could actually do this.

And as if he had seen my thoughts, he let go of my hands and came around the desk. He took a pillow out of a nearby chair and dropped it on the floor.

"Turn your chair," he said, and I did. He knelt on the pillow and lifted my skirt. I spread my legs for him, glad I had put on fresh panties.

"Close your eyes and picture her. Do not worry about the picture being accurate, just concentrate on it."

You may as well know that I love cunnilingus. I love all kinds of sex, and I've tried about everything there is, but a good tongue ... well, there's nothing like it. I remember thinking to myself this was not the craziest thing I'd ever done, but it was the craziest reason anyone ever gave me to do it.

He began by putting his mouth against me and blowing his breath through my damp panties, and the warmth washing over me made me open my legs even farther.

I lay back in the chair and closed my eyes. I have always had a vivid imagination and it was easy to see Martha standing in the choir loft with all her friends, singing. I slunk down a little and pushed my hips forward against Mr. Carlton's mouth, and I swear I saw her face twitch and the sheaf of music in her hands tremble slightly.

I felt something new inside me then; an emotion I had never felt before and couldn't give a name to. It was as powerful as sex and just as exciting. I pushed his head away then and brought my knees together so I could wriggle out of my panties. Then I scrunched way down so I was just on the edge of the chair, and put my legs over the padded arms so I was wide open for him.

And as his tongue began to dance in just the right spot, and the hot little flashes started shooting up, I saw Martha gasp in the middle of a long high note.

The more excited I got, the clearer the picture of her became. She was looking nervously from side to side now as her face got redder, and I saw she had a little beauty mark on her left cheek.

I kicked off my shoes and put my feet around the back of Mr. Carlton's head. "Inside," I told him, "put your tongue inside."

He did, and his tongue felt impossibly long and thick, and so good that I started moaning, and I could feel/see/hear Martha trying to stifle the sound in her own throat.

As soon as the song ended, she excused herself. She practically ran down the stairs to the ladies' room in the basement. She thought the funny feeling meant she had to pee real bad. Frantically, she pulled up her dress and pulled down her panty hose and underwear and sat down on the toilet. That's when I grabbed Mr. Carlton's head with my hands and held him hard against me. I remember as I/she came thinking that it was too bad she wasn't with everybody, that I would have loved to have seen the horrified looks of everybody around her.

I'm one of those rare women who gush when they come hard, and Mr. Carlton, PBS butler supreme, had the kind of expert tongue and lips that made me flood his mouth like a bursting dam. Being the perfect gentleman, he drank up every drop. God, he was good! He was so good that Martha slid backward and whacked her head on the toilet tank in the ladies' room. I know it hurt, because I felt it too. I was still rubbing my head as he stood up.

"Well?" He was wiping his face with a white linen handkerchief and smiling.

"I think it was good for all of us," I said grinning.

"I knew it. You are incredible, my dear. And quite delicious."

33

"Thank you, Mr...., ah ... Ross. You're pretty good yourself."
I stood up then, and got my panties. I turned my back as I
pulled them up and stepped into my shoes. My face was on
fire, but I felt happy.

"I'm glad. You have also made an old man very happy," he
said.

⁂

Of course, all the way home I was arguing with myself, and by
the time I got there I had talked myself into believing that
what had just happened hadn't really. My left brain couldn't
accept it, and kept telling me that it had all just been a just a
crazy way for an old man to get a little young pussy.

Meanwhile, my right brain kept flashing the lifelike pictures of Martha's face, all screwed up and gasping with terror
and joy as she experienced her first orgasm.

I was very confused and called June. She came over right
away.

⁂

"God, Marge! I can't believe that of all people, you would fall
for something like this!"

"Yeah, it sounds pretty crazy, doesn't it. And yet, I'm still
not sure. It was so clear, and I could feel and hear her too."

"Christ, he could have done anything to you! What if he
had been some kind of nut? He could have tied you up, and
carried you down to some dark room in the basement and..."

"And cut me up into little pieces? You've been watching
too much television. Besides I like being tied up, and so do
you."

"But even so, he was so old! How could you stand it?"

"I keep telling you that older men are better, Junie. They
have experience. They know how to treat a girl. Ross certainly
knew what he was doing with his tongue."

"Ugh, don't talk about it! It gives me the creeps! And sucking him must have been disgusting. How could you!"

"He didn't ask me to. In fact he didn't want anything from me. All he did was to make me promise to let him know what happened. He didn't even want any money. I offered but he actually seemed offended. Then I left, that's all."

Actually, that wasn't all. He had kissed me good-bye at the door, and his lips had felt as nice as his hands, young and strong and passionate. I don't think anyone had ever kissed me quite like that. It wasn't a long kiss but so thorough it made me dizzy.

I didn't tell Junie that part because she wouldn't have understood. She has always gone after younger guys. She likes the tough, hot stud types, guys who wear leather and think they're the answer to every woman's dreams. And although she loves oral sex with me, she's not really keen on sucking cock. I know her boyfriends make her do it, and she likes it when they get a little rough and force her, and she's probably great as far as they're concerned because they know so little, but I know she doesn't have her heart in it.

I know because I've seen her take on a bunch of guys back when we used to have our "parties" in high school. She was OK as long as she was getting fucked, but without a cock ramming hard up inside her she loses her enthusiasm for what she has in her mouth. Don't get me wrong—she loves sex as much as I do, but she just isn't a born cocksucker.

"And you really think Martha felt it?" she asked.

"I don't know. It sure felt real. I wish there was some way to find out." That's when I got my wonderful idea.

"Hey, what are you doing Sunday?"

She looked at me blankly for a minute, then she said, "Oh no! No you don't! No, no, no, no!"

But I knew she would. After all, what are friends for?

And just like I knew she would, Junie started thinking it was fun once she got into it. She even came over early that Sunday on her way to church and was giggling as she hiked up her somewhat tight but otherwise suitably conservative dress to show me the sexy garter belt and stockings she had on. Of course she wasn't wearing anything else.

"There's no reason you should be having all the fun," she giggled. June was raised Catholic like me, and has been struggling with it ever since too. We were both rebellious types even in elementary school, and the nuns and the priest used to hold our hands behind our backs when we had to lay over their laps to be spanked.

We both got to like it, and Junie especially would get into trouble hoping it would be Father Martin. She went to see him right after graduation and somehow convinced him to do it one last time. It scared the hell out of him when she came, and even though we'd both gone well beyond spankings, we still used him as a benchmark: "Well, how was (name of new boyfriend)?" one of us would ask, and the other would say, "Oh, about a (number) on the Father Martin scale" (on which he is a ten), and we'd laugh.

Tommy, who was no Father Martin, but a lot more dependable, had already shown up and was drinking coffee in my bed, waiting for me. Tommy is one of those rare males that can be a friend and/or a lover without getting sticky about it. Maybe it's because he's bisexual.

We've known him for a long time, and both of us have slept with him lots of times. Every girl that lives alone has a night once in a while when she feels lonely and horny, and not really in the mood for going out or for romance and all the rest of that stuff. All she wants is to be thoroughly fucked and go to sleep. It's like taking a sleeping pill, only better.

That's when I would call up Tommy. He's good-looking and not real bright, but he's great in bed, and doesn't talk too much or say stupid things afterwards. He just gets dressed and smiles and waves good-bye and goes home, and sometimes that was just what I wanted.

And when June feels blue, she calls Tommy to snap her out of it. Tommy knows what she likes, and her limits and she trusts him. He may not be a rocket scientist, but he *is* an expert with ropes and leather.

He has this gym bag of stuff he carries around with him in his car, and he knows more knots and tricks with ropes then you can imagine. June loves all the different ways he ties her up, and that he knows just how hard to hit her with the strap or the paddle to make her come.

She can come just from the feeling of being totally restrained, and loved to have Tommy and I next to her fucking while she wiggled against her ropes, and the sound of her moaning through her gag would set both of us off too.

Sometimes I just sprawled in the chair and got myself off watching them, and sometimes I joined in and let him tie me up too. There is something about being totally helpless that sets you completely free. I still like it a lot.

Well, that's who Tommy is, and that's why he was the perfect choice for our little experiment. Also, he didn't ask a lot of questions.

I had described Martha to June and had told her about what time we would start. I wanted to wait until they were in the middle of the service, so Tommy and I just took it slow at first, building it up so that it would be a really good one. Thank God Henry was still out of town, so he wasn't there that Sunday. He would have recognized June and wondered what the hell was going on.

God, men are funny. They're all so different from one another and yet they're all the same. Take cocks, for instance. Tommy has one of those long thin ones, the kind that never gets totally steel hard. Whenever he put it in my cunt I always wanted it to be a little thicker, like Henry's, but then he compensated for it by making it jerk inside so it felt like a live snake. Where I really liked his cock was in my ass. It always felt so perfect up there. That was another reason why I was so happy he could come over. I had figured that this would really freak out Martha.

We sucked and licked each other in a lazy 69 for a while until it was time. It was nice, like a Sunday-morning breakfast in bed, except without the crumbs. I kept looking at my watch, so Tommy knew something was up, but after I told him to mind his own business, he stopped asking. Then, as I got more and more excited I began to hear the music, and that was nice too. It made it kind of mystical. Since I think that sex is one of the most mystical things you can do, the sound of a church organ seemed that much more appropriate.

As soon as I closed my eyes and concentrated I could see/feel/hear her clearly. It was almost like I was inside her and yet floating up in the air just over her at the same time. I couldn't see her face very well and so I moved. I don't know how I did that, but I thought it and it happened.

I waited until she got up to sing and then handed Tommy the KY from the table next to the bed. I got up on my knees, and shivered as his wiggling fingers greased me. Then seeing the look on Martha's face made it even better. Tommy is very considerate, and usually he takes it easy, working his cock in slow and letting me get used to it, but I wasn't sure how long the song would last, and besides this time I was already ready.

"Now, Tommy. Stick it in all the way!" I said.

He did, and it was like lava inside. If this was really happening, I thought, Junie had to see the way it made Martha jump.

"Fuck me hard, Tommy," I told him, wanting it so badly it didn't matter what Martha was feeling.

Of course, the guy has to know what he's doing, but any woman that hasn't had a man's dick slithering around up there is missing half the joy of sex. It's still fucking, but with a different flavor to it, rich and tangy like a good dark chocolate ice cream instead of smooth and subtle and slippery like vanilla. Except that it's hot instead of cold.

Well, mixed metaphors aside, it wasn't long before Tommy's cock had me facedown, biting the sheets. I kept urging him to do it faster and harder as I rubbed my clit and pinched my nipples. I didn't ascribe anything to it until a long time later, but I don't think I ever came so hard in my life. It was like the top of my head was being blown off.

It made Martha faint.

I was still asleep later when June burst in. Strangely, the sex had knocked me out instead of making me feel lively. Tommy had already gone.

"Wow, it was great! Everybody else thought she was sick, or having a fit, but I was watching her face, and I could tell what it was! They had to stop everything and cart her off," she said.

Although I heard her, it was far away, and I could barely keep my eyes open. It was like I had fainted too.

"Hey, are you OK, Margie? Jesus, you look beat!"

"Well, I do feel a little groggy. And sore too. Tommy really got into it there at the end. No pun intended."

"I think *you* need a shower," she said, giggling, and pulling me out of bed and toward the real reason I had chosen this apartment to rent: the large, modern shower/bathtub combination, because I love taking long hot showers and relaxing baths. Also it was a great place to play with friends.

I had June hold the shower massage on my back where Martha had whacked herself when she fell. The stinging needle spray helped take away some of the ache. Then I had her use it on my ass, and she held my cheeks apart and used the pulsing spray and it helped the throbbing.

"Do you think you really did it, Margie?" she asked.

"You were there. You saw what happened."

"Yeah, and when I saw it I believed it. But now, I don't know. It's just too weird. It could have been a coincidence."

Actually, I didn't want to believe it myself. I mean it's one thing to wish your enemies harm; it's another to have the power to make your wishes come true!

"Well, even if it didn't," she said a few minutes later, "it got *me* all hot. You've had your fun, now how about some for me?"

I took the sprayer from her then, and sat down as she stood over me and held her cunt open. I teased her with the medium setting she likes best, and after she came I tasted her, and that got me excited again, and we dried each other and got into bed and her tongue made me forget all about what had happened, and how good, and at the same time how scared, it had made me feel.

But after she left, I thought about it some more and decided that "scared" was not quite the right word. I remember it was more like a mixture of awe that maybe I could really do this, dread of what being able to do this might do to *me*, and, unbelievably, concern about what I was doing to Martha.

I realized then that I was starting to feel a little sorry for her. I guess whatever this connection was, it was allowing me to get to know her, and I was discovering that she was, as they say in the song, "more to be pitied then censured."

I was very confused, to say the least. I didn't believe it was magic, and I still don't. If there was such a thing we'd all be busy turning each other into toads, and turning ourselves back into ourselves.

Then I started thinking about Henry, the man I was doing this all for. He was coming back on Tuesday, and I would see him as soon as he got in, because he had told Martha that he wasn't coming back until Wednesday night. I couldn't decide whether I should tell him or not, and I sure as hell didn't know what to say if I did: "Hi, Henry. Hey, honey, I've got some great news! While you were away I figured out how to drive your wife crazy. I make her come in church!"

I realized then this was going to be more complicated than I thought. But later that night, around midnight, it got even worse. That's when Martha called me for the second time.

"I don't know how you did it, but I know it's you. Please stop. Please...," she said, and her voice was plaintive and soft, and then she hung up.

The dial tone was like a machine somewhere howling in endless pain. It meant something, and I listened to it until the sound changed to those awful high-pitched beeps of outrage and forced me to hang up. It was then I decided to stop.

When Henry came home everything seemed to return to normal, at least for a while. And then things started getting really crazy. I found myself waking up in the middle of the night on my knees by the side of my bed with my hands together in front of my face.

As I said, I don't believe in God anymore, but if I did, I would never be so stupid and egotistical to think that prayer meant anything. I mean suppose for a minute He is out there, seeing and knowing everything. He has to take care of five billion of us every second, plus the sun and the stars and the millions of other galaxies and black holes and cosmic strings, whatever they are, so how could he possibly have time to listen to any one of us? And why to me? And why would he want to?

And not only that, but if he made it all, why is so much of it bad? Why is there so much pain and suffering in the world?

I know these are little-kid questions. I asked them when I was a kid in Sunday school, and I never liked the answers I got. I still don't: "That's where faith comes in."

"We are not meant to understand everything."

"God moves in mysterious ways."

What bullshit!

41

And don't think I gave up right away either. I've studied the "problem of evil" on and off for years. It wasn't in my catechisms, so I read Thomas Aquinas, and then a whole lot of others, and then all about other religions, and for a while in college I even fancied myself a Zen Buddhist like everybody else.

But finally I realized that despite all their complex constructs and their logical intricacies, and despite how much it taught me, all these people didn't have the answers either, and that all of it wasn't much different than "Cinderella," and that much of it was actually a hell of a lot dumber.

Anyway, every time the praying happened, it scared me more then anything that had ever happened to me. And not just because I was doing it, I'd done it enough times when I used to think it worked, but because of the way it made me feel this time—like I was losing myself, like little pieces of me were drifting away into space, and that had never happened before.

I could almost see them, like the tiny bubbles in a glass of soda, racing to the top and then, instead of bursting, flying up into the air and happily drifting around the ceiling. That's not really what I saw, but that's the best metaphor I can think of to describe it.

And worst of all, I loved it while it was happening. I wanted the effervescence to go on and on until there was nothing left of me. That's what really scared me. That, and because I knew Martha was doing it to me.

I didn't even have to tell Junie something was wrong. She could tell right away from the way I was acting.

She had bought herself a new vibrating dildo and we were in her bed trying it out. I had strapped it on first, and put the little vibrating ball that ran off the same batteries up inside me, and it and the big lifelike cock were both humming away as I fucked her.

Well, she got off right away, but I didn't, so I got on my knees and Junie put it on and started fucking me with it. It felt really good, but it must have been obvious my mind was elsewhere because after ten minutes Junie said, "What's the matter, sweetie?"

"It's Martha. I think she's trying to get back at me."

"Martha? I thought you had decided to leave her alone. What's she doing?"

"She's making me pray."

"Jesus, how awful! What are you going to do about it?"

"I don't know."

"Well, don't think about now, honey. Just try to relax and enjoy this. I know I am," she said.

I closed my eyes and tried, and suddenly it was as if Martha were behind me instead of June, and we weren't in bed but kneeling together side by side in church. It sounds corny, but it was dark, and there was this holy light around the two of us and it wasn't a cold dark, but warm and enveloping like we were being held in ancient invisible hands. I felt safe and happy, and then she turned and looked at me, but it wasn't her head that had moved or her eyes that were staring at me. It was something inside her that was seeing something inside me. She reached out for me without moving her arms, and she touched me without using her fingers and in that moment I felt there was no good and bad in the world and I understood what I was for, and I started to drift apart like smoke.

I think I would have disappeared if I hadn't come. It was so powerful, so complete that it is impossible to describe, and Junie felt it too.

"Wow, what was that?" she asked me when we had both recovered enough to talk. "It was like your orgasm traveled right through the dildo and up inside of me!"

Already the whole thing was getting too unreal to put into words. "I don't know, but I'm going to find out," I said.

43

As soon as I got home I called up Mr. Carlton. Again he seemed to know what was going on, and he told me to come right over even though it was pretty late. I took a quick shower and jumped in the car, leaving the windows open to dry my hair. I had trouble finding a place to park this time, and had to walk two blocks to get to his house.

He opened the door when I was only halfway up the steps. He was dressed in a long old-fashioned quilted robe—dark purple with a white silk ascot at his throat—and looked this time like he was the lead in one of those seduction scenes from a '30s movie. He even had a cigarette in one of those long black holders, and when we went into his office the smoke started drifting around his head like it was supposed to. He handed me a tall bubbling glass of champagne. This time the gloves he wore were thin expensive black leather. Once again we had one of those strange conversations.

"Well, Margaret? Are things working out for you and Henry?"

"I guess. I mean we still love each other."

"Guessing again, are we?"

"Well, it's not Henry. It's Margaret. She's starting to do things back."

"What things?"

"It hard to describe. She's trying to make me, ah, disappear."

"How?"

"By praying. And by ... by making me pray."

"Ah, I thought as much."

"What do you mean?"

"Well, it makes sense. It is what she knows how to do. It's the only thing she really knows how to do, and she does it very well. She ought to. She's been doing it all her life."

"You sound like you know her."

"Oh, I do. She's a client. Like you. She was referred to me by her priest. Father O'Hurleahy."

"What! You mean after you helped me, you started helping her too?"

"No, as a matter of fact, I knew her long before I met you. She has been having her problems for quite a while. Seeing things and hearing voices when she prayed. First her grandparents, then her mother and father. I did some research. Her descriptions were very accurate."

"Accurate? Well, why shouldn't they be?"

"Because Martha was brought up by foster parents. All her relatives were killed in the war in London. In the blitz. She was a newborn baby when it happened. She never knew them."

"God, that's awful. But still, that doesn't mean you should be doing what you're doing. You're playing both ends against the middle! You should have told me!" He set down his glass then and stood very close to me.

"Told you what, my dear?"

He was smiling and his eyes were doing their thing again. And when he began caressing my cheek with one finger, I couldn't move.

"What you're doing," I said, trying to be angry, but his touch had drained it all away.

"And what is it I'm doing?"

He started moving his hands over my neck and shoulders, and all the tension and resentment left me too.

"I don't know," I said. And I really didn't.

"I'm helping you, that's what I'm doing. Now drink your champagne."

I did, and he took my empty glass and set it down next to his. Then he held my face in his gloved hands like it too was a fragile, long-stemmed glass, and his kiss made me bubble inside, and my knees go weak.

It was impossible to think, and I let him lead me to the couch. I had put on my black dress with the big zipper that goes from my neck to my knees, and as he slowly unzipped it, the whispering sound of it, the gradual way it revealed me, I knew it was because he had wanted me to wear it.

As usual, I wasn't wearing a bra, and the way he kissed my breasts, as tenderly as he had kissed my mouth, made me tremble. Then he slid my panties down and nuzzled and kissed me there too as he knelt to take them off. Then I had to hold onto his head as he slipped off the high heels I had put on because they went with the dress, and the way he kissed my feet so I felt like I was being worshipped, it made me feel even more helpless and excited.

"I think it's time we introduced Martha to something new, don't you?" he said, standing again. "Lie down on your tummy. Crossways," he said, and his voice made it impossible not to obey him.

The couch was one of those armless ones like analysts have in their offices. The leather felt incredible on my belly and breasts, the cool shock of it warming up immediately so it was like someone else's skin.

He had put a pillow on the floor for my knees, and then he was tying my ankles together with his silk ascot. He brought my hands together behind my back, and I watched him over my shoulder as took the handcuffs out of the pocket of his robe and put them on me.

The little clicking sounds, the coolness of the metal on my wrists sent little hot flashes from my cunt to my brain. I knew he had planned this all out, and I remember thinking about what June said, that I didn't know this man at all; but the adrenaline rush I felt wasn't fear. This man knew just what to do to excite me, and he was about to offer me limitless possibilities, and this was why it was impossible to resist him.

He took off his robe, revealing tight black leather pants with a cut-out front, and high slim black leather boots that matched the gloves he still had on. His pale cock was as smooth as a baby's, and even though it was only half hard, it was long and dangled wonderfully in front of my eyes. I had never seen a man with white pubic hair before. It had the same no-color, every-color iridescence as the snowy hair on his head, and the rest of him was as smooth and naked as a baby too, and he had a better shape then most younger men, and now I knew that whatever it was he had planned I wanted it too.

He unbuckled the wide belt and slid it out of the loops of his pants. "Are you ready? Are you concentrating on her?"

I closed my eyes.

Martha was sitting in her living room sewing. The television was on, some talk show on one of the religious channels. Henry wasn't in the room, and it didn't seem like he was in the house.

"Don't you think we ought to warn her?" I said.

He went and got the telephone. He punched her number, and held the handset for me.

"Martha, this is Margaret. What are you doing right now?"

"Watching television. Why? How dare you call me! What do you think..."

"Shut up. This is important. Is Henry home?"

"No."

"Good, I want you to get undressed and go to bed. Now."

"What?"

"You heard me. Do it."

"Oh, God! Not again! Please..."

"This is for making me pray, Martha." I looked at Mr. Carlton and nodded. He hung up.

"We'll have to give her a few minutes," I said.

He was still holding the phone. "While we wait, my dear, I wonder if you'd mind..."

I had wanted to ever since he took the robe off. "I thought you'd never ask," I said.

He moved closer and bent his knees. Unlike Junie, I love the taste and feel of a man's cock in my mouth. It's his most vital part, and it makes me feel powerful and powerless at the same time; like you feel when you're holding an infant. And I love the way they change: first they're soft and small and undemanding, like those little gumdrop candies you roll around on your tongue to get the sugar off; then they get longer and thicker as they get springy, and finally, hard and insistent, leaking their little love drops, they take on their final, unique shapes.

Size is not important. Within limits, of course. I prefer them average, at least as far as fellatio is concerned. I like to be able to get all of a man into my mouth once he's erect.

Like I said before, men are all different and yet all the same, and their cocks are as distinctive as fingerprints, or earlobes. Mr. Carlton's was straight and smooth, the head not much bigger then the rest. And despite his age, he got very hard very quickly. I took it as a compliment, and it got me even more excited.

And the excitement made it even easier to see/feel/hear Martha. She was undressing hurriedly, the tears streaming down her face. I was surprised how nice she looked naked. She seemed to have actually gotten prettier. She had nice cupcake breasts, and was round and soft at the hips like a Rubens painting. I thought she could use some help with her hair though.

She got out a clean flannel nightgown from her dresser, and I said, *Unh-uh,* mentally and that scared her even more, and she put it back. She was shaking and sobbing as she pulled the blankets down, but then suddenly she dropped down on her knees and started praying.

Startled, I pulled my head back. Mr. Carlton straightened up.

"Now! Do it now!" I said. Already I could feel her pulling at me.

He moved quickly around to the other side of the couch and picked up the belt.

I always cringe for the first few blows, until the burning on my skin begins melting me inside. If you've never done this, don't let anybody tell you that it doesn't hurt. It does, but suddenly the way it hurts changes. Just like we all want to believe in something, we all want to stop believing in anything, and when you cross that threshold between pain and pleasure, when you can't tell the difference anymore, all the dichotomies you live by start to crumble, and you forget who you are, and sometimes that can be pretty wonderful.

Mr. Carlton was as good with the belt as he had been with his tongue. When you do this to somebody, you have to want to hurt them, but you have to care about them too. I've always found it best to pretend that it's me I'm hitting, and as long as you're a fairly normal human being, which means that you both love and yet need to punish yourself once in a while, you'll know just how hard to hit your lover.

In minutes he had my juices flowing, and they, and the sheen on the rest of me, allowed me to slide and wiggle around on the deliciously hot couch. God, it was great, the two kinds of leather doing two different kinds of great things to me both at the same time!

Martha had screamed and grabbed at her ass when it started. And she kept holding her hands there, still trying furiously to pray. But then as each blow of the belt brought me closer and closer, she drew her hands up and clasped them behind her back so they were like mine, and she started moaning right along with me.

I can sometimes come just from being tied up and whipped. It makes me crumble inside, until there's only tiny pieces left, and then it builds me back up until I'm at the brink, but usually I need to be fucked or have my cunt licked or have my clit rubbed.

Amazingly, Martha helped. She started fingering herself, and I could hear/feel her wishing that Henry's cock was sliding into her cunt. I should have been jealous, but I wasn't, because it was what I wanted too.

We achieved simultaneous orgasm, like they always do in the movies, but it wasn't just two at the same time at a distance, it was the same one, and it was twice as powerful because we were sharing it.

I must have blacked out because the next thing I remember was Mr. Carlton saying my name softly, and I felt a damp coolness on my back and on the burning skin of my ass. Then I heard what I thought were bells until I finally realized it was the water tinkling in a little metal basin each time he dipped the washcloth and wrung it out.

"Welcome back," he said. He had already removed the knotted ascot from my ankles.

"Not yet," I told him, when he put the key in the handcuffs.

"Don't you think she's had enough?"

"Not for her. For you. And for me."

He kissed my back. "Margaret, you are truly one of the most sexual beings I have ever met," he whispered.

He spread my legs and knelt between them. He kept kissing my shoulders and neck the whole time he was fucking me, and then he was biting me just hard enough at just at the right moment, and it made it even better, so that this time there was just him and me, and I swear I could feel him coming inside me.

The next day the warfare between us broke out into the open. Henry came over to see me, and said he was sure that Martha was going crazy, that she had dragged him into bed last night, and—he actually said these words—"fucked his brains out," that she had had an orgasm, and had said afterwards it was all my fault.

I had to tell him then. I knew he would think I was crazy too, but I hate lying. I do it when I have to, because society demands it, but I hate it, and I couldn't lie to him.

As soon as you tell the first one to the one you love, you put the first brick in the wall between you. I know that sounds old-fashioned, but it's how I feel. So when I told him, I told him *everything*. He was stunned.

He came back the next day. He had called in sick. He told me he needed time to think, and had already taken some of his stuff from home and gotten himself a rented room.

I stood watching him, on the edge of tears, unable to say anything, knowing it wouldn't do any good anyway, as he packed up the few things he had kept at my place. It was obvious it was tearing him apart inside just like it was doing to me.

The little cardboard boxes he was using made me realize how he had compartmentalized his life. He had his job, he had his wife, and he had me, and he had been managing by keeping them separate. Now he couldn't anymore, and he didn't know what to do.

I guess to some degree all of us are like that. I remember in college being taught the theory of cognitive dissonance, that when a person has two contradictory thoughts, a psychological tension is produced that drives the person crazy until they can figure out some way to reduce it. The theory is nice, but in practice I've found that most people either convince themselves there is no contradiction, or they manage very easily not to think about the two things at the same time.

Men seem to be particularly adept at this. They can be one thing at work, and entirely something else at home. And then they go to their clubs, or go out with the guys and are yet another person entirely. Of course, society, and, to be honest, us women, not only encourage men to do this, we damn well demand it.

Society doesn't ask that of women. What we're being told is that we have to have a home, *and* a career, *and* kids, *and* a lover on the side, and be slim, and pretty and youthful while still being honest and natural. Jesus, it's a wonder we're not all schizophrenic!

Henry had never made those kinds of demands on me. He had just wanted me to be myself. When he was with me, he was *with* me, and now I realized that when he was with Martha, he was *with* her. It explained why he was always reluctant to talk about her, and why, when I had insisted, his voice would get low and he'd drop off the ends of his sentences.

And I had been doing the same thing—loving Henry in the "now," as if the future didn't exist; not believing in magic and yet practicing "body voodoo" on Martha.

What kept me going at that point was that quote of F. Scott Fitzgerald: "The test of a first rate intelligence is the ability to hold two opposed ideas in the mind at the same time and still retain the ability to function."

I was still functioning after Henry left, but only just barely. I decided it was time to ask for a truce. I picked up the phone, but the mindlessness of the dial tone stopped me, and I hung up. It was time that we met face-to-face.

I drove past the house slowly, trying to see in the windows, suddenly worried that Henry had lied or changed his mind and gone back. But his car wasn't there and I circled the block and parked a little way up the street. I could tell she was there; I don't know how, but I knew.

They lived in one of those very nice houses in one of those expensive suburban neighborhoods. I had seen pictures of it once, but seeing it for real was a shock, and suddenly the life that Henry lived with Martha seemed real, and it made her more real and my life with Henry less so.

Henry had taken the pictures because Martha had had some landscaping done, some bushes taken out and moved and flowers put in. But he had left the roll of film with me to be developed before he went out of town because it also had some pictures of me on his boat.

In one of them, I was naked, standing up on the boom and leaning back against the sail. The wind had been blowing hard and steady that day and the boat was heeled over, doing a sweet and steady seven knots up the bay, and I just couldn't resist stripping off my suit and climbing up there.

I still remember what it was like, the warm humid salt air like God's tongue all over me, and the other boats just far enough away so maybe they could see me if they looked, and maybe not.

"Hey, naked sailing, what a great idea!" Henry had shouted, taking off his suit too. I couldn't help but play with myself, and the camera caught me just as I was starting to come. It's one of my favorite pictures.

I love sailing. The freedom of it, the way it puts you in touch with the wind, the water, the sky, and the sun; the way it puts you in touch with yourself.

It has always affected Henry that way too. At work or fixing things, or trying to solve a problem, he's an engineer. But on his boat he's a poet, making up little things right on the spot. And they're good too, sometimes funny, sometimes sad. And because of me, he claims, more often than not, romantic or erotic.

He once said that I belonged on a sailboat, that I made him feel as happy as the boat when the wind was just right and the water flat, when she was perfectly balanced moving through the water with her sails hard and quiet. Sometimes he sings when it's like that. Not singing exactly, but chanting, in tune with the hum of the rigging, and in rhythm with the boat, and then I love him so much I can hardly stand it.

Martha had sailed with him when they were first married, but she didn't like it, and stopped going. And sitting in the car then, I thought about never going sailing with Henry anymore, and it was that that made me finally get out and walk up to ring the bell.

"Somehow I knew it was you even before I opened the door," Martha said, her eyes red from crying.

"Can I come in, Martha? We have to talk."

"Of course. But I don't have much time. It's Thursday. As you know, I go to choir practice."

We went into her living room and sat down at some distance from each other. It was almost impossible not to be at a distance in that house; the rooms were huge, the expensive, conventional furniture all spread out. The place looked like it had been done by a confused decorator who couldn't make up her mind whether she liked Early American or Colonial better, and had finally given up and decided to make the place look like anybody could have lived there.

It was about what I had expected, but Martha wasn't. I had seen her as bigger, more imposing. But in person she reminded me of June, small and cute and round and vulnerable. She looked younger too, and her hair was shorter and prettily curled in at the bottom so it framed her face. And then there was the way she was dressed—white silk blouse unbuttoned at the throat and worn loose over tight black slacks. And barefoot, with her toenails painted.

She was Martha, of course, but I realized then that either she had changed or my visions of her had been distorted by what I wanted her to be.

"I didn't expect you to look so pretty," she said finally.

"What?" I had been staring at her, and when she echoed my thoughts, it set me back.

"I guess I pictured you as one of those gum-chewing, slutty types. You know, bleached hair and lots of makeup and wearing skimpy black leather. You're not like that at all."

"No. Well, sometimes. Sometimes I wear clothes like that. Henry likes it."

"Yes. I can see now why he likes you. You are sexy, but in a nice way. As if there was nothing wrong with it."

"There isn't, Martha."

"Well, I've been trying. I got my hair done. What do you think?" She turned her head and lifted her curls. "I even got a pedicure!" She looked down at her feet like a little girl, lifting them together and pointing her toes. Her feet were small and cute like Junie's.

Then she started crying. I got up and sat next to her on the couch and put my arm around her. It was the natural thing to do. Women comfort each other. Even when they're enemies.

"I thought it would help, but it just made everything worse. Henry thinks I've gone crazy," she sobbed.

"Me too," I said, and the tears began running down my cheeks. "I don't know what I'm going to do without him."

"Neither do I-I-I!" she bawled. And then she was holding on to me.

She was warm and soft against me, and it just felt like the most natural thing in the world to lift her face from my shoulder and kiss her. And then she was kissing me back, and we took off each other's clothes and made love right there on the couch.

She was afraid at first, but I showed her how not to be, and she loved it in the end as much as I did.

And afterwards, she asked me to kneel next to her, and that seemed natural and right too.

This time she was with me, and she taught me how to let go, how not to be afraid of the dissolving. It was like making love to her had been, and this time it was as if we were joined for a while somewhere else.

That's the best way I can describe it. It's all metaphor, but I've come to realize that our whole lives, and maybe even all of us, are metaphors for something else.

We eventually got Henry back. He was right: we *are* both crazy. But we convinced him that he was crazy too, and now the three of us live together in a little house outside the city, near the marina, where nobody knows us. We love each other and we share each other. We sleep together and go to church together and sail together. Yes, I go to church again now, and Martha's back sailing.

And sometimes we have our fights too, and then we try to help each other. It's difficult sometimes, because of the times we live in, and how we've all been brought up, but then there *are* crazier ways to live.

And what have I learned from all this?

That our society, or any society, is wrong when it denies what we are. That we are all sexual beings, and we were meant to be that way. And that we are all spiritual beings, and that we were meant to be that way too. There are many sides to each of us, and even though the world tells us different, we must try not to deny any of them, because that's how we connect to each other and to ourselves.

And, even more profoundly, that either paradoxes are the only truths, or that everything that is true at one time and place in the universe is simultaneously as equally untrue in another.

Take God for instance. If He's everywhere, he's also nowhere.

Or love. Everybody wants it; everybody goes out looking for it, and all the time it's inside us.

Or take magic. Either there is no such thing, or everything is magical already and we just don't know it.

There *are* limitless possibilities, and that's enough for my soul. At least for *this* lifetime.

Jack-a-roe

Raven Kaldera

"What do you think?" Rabinowitz asked her, checking his watch. It was nearly two on a Thursday and he was probably late for his golf game, Rachel thought to herself. "Is it worth taking to an appraiser, or do you care about its value?"

She sniffed and wiped her hand across her nose—damn head cold—and looked at the letter in her hand again. "I wouldn't send for an appraiser if it was valuable, Jonathan. This stuff was sent to me for religious—spiritual—reasons." He lifted an eyebrow and she sighed. "Hell, it's as if your great-grandfather sent you a five-century-old shofar from Jerusalem."

The lawyer snorted. "If something like that arrived in the mail, I'd assume it was stolen and return it to Israeli Antiquities before they knocked my door down, But if you don't care, it'll save us all time and money. Four boxes, then. I'll have the other three delivered to your house, and then we'll be free of the business." He hesitated. "I'm sorry, Rachel. I didn't mean to sound like that, not so soon after your great-aunt's death. Were you two close?"

"No, never met her. She wrote the occasional letter from East Germany, but I never talked to her until the Wall came down. Then she got a job with the phone company and started calling all her relatives, all over the world." Rachel grinned at the memory. "Sometimes in the middle of the night. 'Ya, liebchen, talk to Brigitte now,'" she mimicked the accent. She neglected to mention to her pragmatic college friend that Aunt Brigitte managed never to call at two in the morning when she sleeping, but when she was awake crying over a lost girlfriend or some other disaster, exactly when she needed an objective, sympathetic outsider. It had been on one of those calls that Rachel had impetuously come out to her aunt, and the older woman had unflappably informed her that Aunt Brigitte's mother's sister Lucie had been "one of those, too, so it is only a family tradition, ya?"

She said good-bye to Jonathan, glad that the huge law firm that had handled Aunt Brigitte's American affairs had sent someone she knew. Five boxes, he had said. Full of old things, family heirlooms. Rachel knew better. Her great-aunt had been a hexe, a witch, one of a coven of several, holding onto the old traditions even in the repression of East Germany. She knew about Rachel's involvement with the women's spirituality movement and had approved, although the political concepts of goddess worship were rather lost on her. "You make poppets, ya? Nein? I send you letter, show you how, eh? Take the bedsheet from your enemy, cut into a poppet just so high, stuff mit read thread, and vhen dey hurt you, you stick the thorns of hawthorn in—you got hawthorn dere in Boston, liebchen?"

No matter how many times Rachel had tried to explain to her about the law of Karma and how spells on others come back to you, it was no use. Aunt Brigitte would just get

58

impatient and fall back into her Prussian German and finally say something like, "You got to protect y'self, after a while you just know vat you can and cannot, ya?" Oh well. One couldn't expect much from a bunch of old women living in Communist Germany, meeting in old warehouses and repeating a litany they probably didn't even understand, making superstitious spells with poppets to fulfill their repressed and petty fantasies. Still, they were the elders, and deserved respect. That was why Rachel was so pleased that some of the family's ritual implements had been left to her.

Box one contained the letter and a list of things—all in German; she'd have to take a dictionary out of the library and translate. It also contained a rather gruesome talisman: a life-sized hand sewn out of kid with a small candle stub burnt down on each finger. Sort of a makeshift Hand of Glory, like from the old demonology books. Ick. She stuck it in the closet, on a top shelf. Time enough to figure out what to do with that later.

The phone rang, and it was Johanna, her roommate and younger cousin. "Zack home yet?" she asked.

"No," Rachel chuckled. "Still over at Mark's place. He barely sleeps here one night a week these days."

"Huh." Silence for a minute. Johanna was a dyke too, and an emancipated minor, barely eighteen and in her second year of college. She was brilliant, and argumentative, and adorably boyish, with her close-cropped hair and torn jeans. "Well, leave him a note and tell him I stop feeding his cat for him as of today. I might want to be gone myself occasionally. Met somebody yesterday."

"I'll tell him, and I'll feed Kittyboo myself if he doesn't come home,"

Rachel promised, and got off the phone. *Might as well. Not like I've had a sex life in almost a year. Seems like everybody in the lesbian community is either taken or celibate. And you*

*never know if you could trust those bisexuals ... Oh well. Such
is life.* She sighed and went for the cans of cat food.

🌿

Boxes two through four arrived by UPS the next morning in
an uproar of excitement. Shimmer and Dot, her two cats,
accompanied by the lethargic Kittyboo, jumped on the boxes,
sniffing wildly until she shooed them away, opening the first
one with a kitchen knife. Box two—the smallest one. Something like a bundle of feathers and nails and twine rolled
together. When she lifted it carefully, it unrolled into a long
macramelike thing. The letter said, "Ein Hexe-Strickleiter."
Hmmm ... some sort of charm, like a Native American medicine thing? The letter continued, saying, "Hangen in der
Schornstein." Huh. Oh well. Next.

Box three—a glass jar with a peeling label marked "Ap-
felmuss" and a rolled, furry bundle. Rachel examined the jar
curiously. It looked like brownish Crisco with dark flecks in it.
Opened, it smelled like rank vegetation, like green corn or
milkweed. "Trank fur die Flucht," said the letter. *Better not
mess with this until I get that dictionary,* she thought, and put
it in the fridge.

The bundle was a pair of fur gloves and a small pouch of
the same fur. It contained a few wooden disks with strange
markings on them. Not even runes or Theban, nothing she
could recognize. Rachel sighed. *Here I've been a practicing
feminist witch for two years, got half the neo-pagan books in
Griffin's Words, and I still don't know what these things are.*
Then she recognized something—the fur that the gloves and
bag were made of—and shrieked, dropping them.

It was very definitely a gray mackerel tabby pattern.

"Ugh! Oh, Aunt Brigitte, how could you!" The idea of
wearing the dead skins of her own cats revolted her. *Oh well,*
she sighed to herself, *what was I expecting? Delicate carved*

chalices and gleaming jeweled athames? Be realistic. As she opened the last box—the largest—she studied the letter in hopes of getting a clue on the contents before another nasty surprise greeted her. The only words that she could make out were something about "das Masken auf Tante Lucie." Oh, this had belonged to her lesbian great-great-aunt! Perfect! Talk about herstory. The other women in the coven would die of envy.

The crumpled German newspaper yielded to show a face leering up at her. It was of carved wood, worn and peeling, framed in tails of black horsehair and large curving horns. A fringed goatee of fur scrap adorned its chin and empty eyes stared up at her. She lifted it gently, shaking her head. *Of all things, a Horned God mask that looks like the traditional devil. At least I hope it is Pan or something. Well, I don't think we'll have much use for this in the women's spirituality group. Maybe it'll look interesting on the wall...* There was something else, though, under the newspaper, something furry. *Please, Goddess, no more dead cats.* No, this seemed like rabbit fur, soft gray and brown, hanging from a strip of leather with two buckles... *Must be a belt,* Rachel thought as she shook it out.

It was a loincloth of leather and furs, and mounted on the front was a large phallus, beautifully carved of smooth bone.

Rachel dropped it in disgust. *So that's what Great-Great-Aunt Lucie left for me. A devil mask and a damned strap-on dildo. How patriarchal and tacky. What, did she chase her girlfriends around with it, pretending to be a man? How ridiculous. Just because I'm a lesbian doesn't mean I use ... those. Well, so much for herstory. Damned if I'm going to tell anyone about this.* In a fit of pique, Rachel gathered up the whole thing and tossed it into the closet.

Darkness, close and reeking with fear and sweat and her own wastes. Four walls, rough brick, so close around her that she couldn't lie flat but had to huddle in the narrow space. *It's been two days since they bricked me up, and the food is running low.* Fear, fear, terror. *They hanged them all, Lud said, Mother and Anna and Gerhardt and all of them, and they burnt my mask, oh, my beautiful mask carved ten generations ago.* Sound of the chickens, clucking in the yard outside, and faint smoke curling from the wattle-and-daub chimney. It had been a beautiful autumn day when they had hidden her in here, but now there was rain on the air. Lud and Marta would have to let her out soon; if the pastor and his damned flunkies didn't come to search the house by tomorrow, they probably wouldn't come at all ... or would they?

O Queen of Erlfame, O Lady of the Moon, I do not want to die, I am the only one of us left! O Horned King, I swear I will make a new mask, a better one, as soon as I am safe, O old gods keep me safe! You are the new Jack-a-roe, Mother said, and when you are old enough you will be the coven Grandmaster, the Man in Black. It is a safety measure. Tongues may be loosened by torture, but never, never have they found the Man in Black, they think he is merely the Devil himself. The Man in Black must never be found—so He is never a man ... the Double Mask has a will of its own, my mother says. It finds its own. Oh, Lud, Marta, let me out, I am sick and frightened and I would rather face the pastor than hide any longer...

Rachel bolted upright in her bed, still trembling. Sweat soaked her body and matted her cropped hair. Damn! Some nightmare. Sun was coming through the windows, and the horned mask leered at her from the dresser. The phallus dangled insolently from beneath it. *Didn't I throw that awful thing in the closet,* she thought vaguely. *No wonder I had nightmares,*

with it staring at me all night. She got dressed quickly, not looking at it, not quite daring to touch it.

As she stumbled out to the kitchen, Zack, her roommate, greeted her with a steaming cup of coffee. "Heard you yelling in there a while ago," he commented. "You OK?"

"Yeah, yeah, I'm all right, just a nightmare," she muttered. "Haven't seen you around in a while. Mark finally kick you out?"

"Nah, just had to feed the cat. So what are you wearing for the party tonight?"

"Party?"

"Remember? Pre-Halloween gay/lesbian/bisexual bash at the Arlington Street Church. Shanna's gig. Costume stuff."

"Oh, yeah." She sighed. "I don't have anything to ... No. Wait." She sniffed and wiped a hand across her nose; the head cold was easing up. "You still got that leather gear you bought once when you were dating that dude Whatsisface?"

"Rocky? Yeah. Not my thing, I found out. Got the jacket and pants in the closet, only worn once. Help yourself."

"Thanks. Might as well do something different. I mean, it is a costume party," she rationalized aloud. *That and the silly mask ought to make a good outfit. If I had time I'd go as something more political—like put on a toga and go as Sappho, maybe ... nah. No time, and besides three people did that last year.* She grabbed some yogurt from the fridge and headed off to her job at the newsstand.

That night she stripped to her skin and pulled a plain black T-shirt over her head. She was out of clean underwear, so she was reaching for Zack's borrowed leather pants when that carved phallus fell off the dresser with a clunk. She reached out and caught the mask before it could follow, and then retrieved the bone thing from the floor. It felt strangely warm in her hand, not cold as it should have been. Tingles ran up and down her arm. "No," she whispered. "No, I don't want to...." But her hands were moving as if independent of her, buckling the belt around her hips and cinching the middle strap between her legs. The fur was feather-soft against her skin. There was a hard ridge on the back of the area where the phallus was attached; it fitted perfectly between her labia and rubbed up against her clit. She took hold of the cock and slid her hand up and down; it seemed to throb in her grip in spite of the bone-hardness, and she suddenly realized she was wet, very wet. Her clit throbbed with its own beat, and slowly, inevitably, the two synchronized.

She slipped the leather pants on over the soft furs and zipped them up. The jacket shrugged on, and then, tentatively she picked up the mask. In the semi-dark it seemed to grin knowingly at her. *Step over the threshold*, it said. *Do it. Do it.*

She lifted it to her face and slipped the horsehair-fringe cap over her head. For one moment, her eyes focused on the night sky outside, at the half-moon gleaming through the window, and then the green fire rose from her groin to drown her.

"Hey!" Zack yelled as the leather-clad figure banged out through the door. "Hey! I thought we were going to share a cab! I'm not ready yet—" He lunged for the door, but caught only a horned silhouette climbing into a taxi under the streetlights.

It has been a long time. I walk the streets, dressed as I once did in the skins of animals. The lights gleam orange and green and the music is pounding as I enter the dance room behind the church, bodies gleaming and glittering and gyrating to the heart-thumping music. Strange, to find a place of my worship on the territory of my enemies, whose ancestors have burnt so many of my priest/esses. Strange, but perfect. The dance is about to begin.

I dance. They dance also, but with wonderment as they gaze upon me. I writhe through the crowd; those I touch become inflamed, ecstatic, filled with the urge to rut, to fall upon each other. The energy builds, and I push it along. Two women squirm on the food table, between the punch bowl and the potato chips, hands in each other's pants. A young man approaches me, dances around me, offering himself. I accept. At my touch he forgets himself, his surroundings, everything but lust, and goes down on his knees to open the zipper on my leather pants and extract my cock. The crowd around screams in delight and they dance more wildly. I take hold of his head by the curly blond hair as he puts his mouth on my sacredness.

My hips swivel in pleasure. I would like another young man behind me, to press his hardness against my ass and fuck me in mancunt or womancunt while this young one uses his skilled mouth on me. I would like a woman with satiny lips to stand over him and slip her tongue into my mouth while my hands hunt down her breasts, her nipples hard between my fingers. I would like a whole row of witches on all fours, legs spread or asses toward the sky, waiting for my communion as it used to be when I was the bringer of joy. I am the one who crosses all boundaries.

I think about calling to the crowd and getting what I want—I could do it, too—but a man in a uniform approaches, angry. He gestures toward the youth on his knees, whose clever tongue is making me arch my back and growl, and he threatens mayhem if we do not stop. I laugh and make My symbol in his direction. Immediately his member is as hard as mine, harder than flesh is meant to be, and demands excruciating relief. He whirls, stricken, and runs for the bathroom. I laugh again, and come in the pretty boy's mouth, a shower of sparks that zap and tingle. He looks up in ecstasy as it runs over his nerve endings like bubbling waterfalls over rounded stones.

A woman approaches me now—sultry, assertive, demanding, dressed in black like a priestess of old. She strokes me, caresses me, and we dance. My hard cock moves between her thighs. She tells me I have incredible balls, to be doing this here. I laugh and tell her I have none at all, which is the truth. She asks if I would like to go to her place before the policeman gets out of the bathroom. I am not worried, since I know the man is sitting on a toilet seat in tears, beating off again and again into the murky water in a vain attempt to make his erection go away, but I would like to fuck her, so I agree.

In the cab on the way to her place, she asks my name. Jack, I tell her, and find her soft breasts with my hands. She does not ask any more questions, and soon we are at her house. Upstairs, on the bed, I put my head in her crotch and eat her, licking warm cunt and sucking on her hard clit, and she grabs my head by the horns and bucks her pelvis like a deer caught in a trap. She is fertile; I can smell it. Not in her body, but in her soul. Some part of her waits longingly to be plowed and sown.

So I do it. I bring my knees up and plunge my cock deep into her. She speaks in tongues and claws at my back. It is often this way with mortals. I come again, spraying her deep inside with golden sparks, and in her orgasm she speaks my Name. For that moment, she knows Me.

As I leave to hail a cab, I look up at her window. What child will she bear me, I wonder? As I wait, she sweeps a mess of clutter off the table by the window and plops down a typewriter with a determined air. Rolling in a fresh sheet of paper, she begins.

I smile and return to the dance. The night is young yet.

Morning seeped in through the cracks in the blinds, and Rachel grunted and pulled the covers back over her head. It was too early to get up, and the bed was far too comfortable. As she lay there, she became aware of a vague horniness, of the kind one often got laying lazily in bed in the morning, and she humped the mattress a little, thrusting the cock between her legs into the crack of the blankets. Not quite satisfied, she reached down into the morass of bedding until she felt its throbbing warmth in her hand and began to stroke it gently.

Then, like a bolt out of nowhere, she realized what she was doing and yelped.

"Ohgodohgodohgod," she moaned, scrambling out from under the covers. There was something ironic about that, but her mind had other things to think about. Memories of last night came flooding back. *That man on the dance floor ... the one in the bathroom—did I go into the men's room or the women's room or both?—and that woman, the one I went home with, she thought I was ... Oh god. She was touching my chest, and she never noticed I had breasts. Or did she just not care? What the hell happened?* Her fingers stumbled over the buckles as she undid the belt and tore it off; there was a faint tearing sensation and her clitoral area felt slightly raw. With a muted, wounded noise, she flung the thing into the corner. The phallus was still decorated with a black latex condom, and when it fell it seemed to lie in wait like the head of a coiled black serpent.

The goat-horned mask lay grinning up at her from the night table, a taunting testament to madness.

Rachel rushed, naked and shivering, into the shower and scrubbed herself practically raw with Zack's loofah sponge. *Ohgodohgod what did I do? There was some sort of orgy in the bathroom at the church, and ohgod I lowered myself onto this guy's dick while he lay on the floor, he was the one who had all the black condoms, and I bent him over the sink and fucked him up the ass, and his friend with the red hair too, and then I fucked two Goth chicks with long black hair, and ohgod there was this bald girl who got down on her knees and licked my*

67

asshole and I thought it was worship—was this all a bad drug trip? Did somebody slip me some acid or something? Was it ... magic?

Real magic?

She spent the day curled up on the couch in her bathrobe gratefully watching mind-numbing soaps, terrified to go into her room. Her head cold was back, and she was sniffling. At four o'clock Johanna got home from her class, breezing cheerily through the door. Her eyebrows went up when she saw Rachel.

"Shit, honey, you OK?" she asked. "You look bad, like the flu or something."

Rachel sighed. Maybe that was it. The head cold had degenerated into flu delirium. Still, she wasn't taking chances. "Do me a favor?" she asked.

"Sure, whatever." The brown eyes in Johanna's gamine face were worried.

"In my room ... there's some old stuff. It'd be good if you could take it to the trash for me." Now that she had asked, she was a little embarrassed at being caught with anything like that ... thing.

"Sure, what is it? I'm just stopping in for a minute though, gotta pack a bag and run, so it can't be a major cleaning job," she cautioned.

"No, no ... just something that got left. A mask, on the night table. And a, a belt, I think, made of fur, that she, uh, dropped in the corner."

"Huh. Not going to return them?"

"No ... don't think anybody wants them, not now." Well, that's true enough. She focused in on *Wheel of Fortune* as Johanna shrugged and went into her room, gym bag casually slung over her shoulder.

Mask. Yeah, there it was. Neat. Old, too. *Looks like an antique,* Johanna mused. *Rachel must be an idiot to throw this away. Since she doesn't want it, I might just do some research and find out if it has any value.* Making a mental note to check the Harvard library tomorrow, she sauntered over to where the pile of fur and black latex lay and picked it up, drawing her breath in sharply.

So this is what bothered Rachel, she thought sardonically. *Someone probably offered to use it on her, and she's such a politically correct prude that she freaked out and threw them out. And is probably still processing to* Wheel of Fortune. *Huh.* She peeled the latex off and turned the phallus over and over in her hand, liking the smoothness. *Nice, for a piece of bone, or is it antler? Harder than my four latex ones, but the harness is a lot nicer. Fur is a neat idea. Bet it feels good, too.*

Lifting it to her face, she rubbed her cheek into the softness and inhaled. It smelled of animal, of sex. Johanna's other hand went inadvertently to her guilty secret, the rolled-up sock she wore compulsively stuffed into her underwear. Men's underwear, although nobody knew that except two girls she had fucked in the past year. Who could possibly throw such a lovely thing away? She unzipped her gym bag and tucked both the harness and the mask in, padded them with two T-shirts and her good silk tie.

Rachel kept her eyes fixed on the TV until Johanna reappeared and headed for the door. "All taken care of," the teenager called back to her. "I'll be gone for the night. Get some rest and drink fluids. You'll get over it." There was an amused tone in her voice that Rachel didn't quite catch. She sighed in relief that it was all over, and she'd never have to deal with it again.

"Thanks," she called after the retreating figure in the bomber jacket and sneakers. "Good luck, Jo."

"I'm always lucky," Johanna called back, shifting the bag from one shoulder to another. It was true. The right stuff always came to her, like a bolt out of nowhere. Almost as if someone was watching, hoping... She shrugged off the feeling and headed toward the bus stop. It was a beautiful autumn day, with just the faintest scent of rain on the air.

I, Slimerod

Albert J. Manachino

It's gotten to the point when I'm barely finished with one assignment when I'm called upon for another. That's what happens when you have a reputation for reliability and craftsmanship. I never fail. I'd like to tell them what they can do with some of these assignments, but I can't. It's against the rules. The customer is always right.

The Wallender case was a tough one. Had to endure weeks of exorcism. But I finally wrapped it up for my client. You'd think after one like that, I'd be entitled to a few winks of sleep, but no! I'm just laying my head down when I experience that feeling of dissolution again. It's sort of a melting away, a sundering of my atoms. I'm being pulled apart like an exploded diagram.

One minute I'm in my snug subterranean cavern enjoying the smell of brimstone and volcanic ashes. The next, I'm in a strange room in the middle of a triangle. There's a black candle on each corner of the triangle, which means a dark magician is doing the calling. As if any other kind would have anything to do with me.

This one is a good-looking guy, pale complexion, sallow face with discolored teeth and a wholesome, sour odor of an unclean mouth. Prominent blackheads. Untidy, greasy hair. Shallow chest ... you know the kind, you see them on the covers of men's magazines all the time.

He's in the middle of a protective circle which means he ain't a complete amateur.

I sound far from gracious. "Okay! What is it?"

Despite the protection, he draws back. I guess he's not too experienced after all. If you're going to be successful as a black magician, you got to exhibit lots of confidence in front of whatever it is you're calling at all times.

"Are ... are you a possessing demon?" He sounds scared.

"What do I look like, an ice cream cone?"

"I ... I don't know. I've never called any of your kind before."

"That's obvious. No! I'm not a demon. I'm an imp of the tenth degree. Possession is my specialty. I got to obey your orders. Now get to the point. Something fast, I wanna get some sleep."

"I order you to possess a woman who has grossly and unjustly insulted me."

"Oh ——!" I say, flinging my hat onto the floor. "Another of those! You mean, she turned you down."

"Yes."

"——!" I say again, "for this I got to lose my forty winks." I gnash my teeth. "All right, I follow you. You want her to come crawling to you on all fours begging for your favors, is that it?"

"No, the insult is too deep to let her off that lightly."

"She laughed at you?"

"If you need to be so blunt ... yes."

"So what am I supposed to do about it?"

"She must suffer and she must know why she's suffering."

"I'll whisper it in her ear."

"Her agony must be prolonged and I want it to terminate in self-destruction. You say you're experienced?"

"References he wants yet. I've never failed. No one has ever been able to exorcise me. Once they tried to drive me out by racking the woman I was possessing. I laughed in their faces. They put her foot in an iron boot and poured melted lead inside of it. You should have heard what I told them they could do to themselves." Pale-face is visibly impressed.

"When did you finally leave her?"

"A couple of days later. She died."

"The woman I want you to possess is a friend of the exorcist Stuart Falcon James. I've heard that he's very good."

"Never heard of him. Exorcists are a dime a dozen. Most of them are fakes or incompetents. Give me the particulars."

"The what? I don't understand."

"Name and address of the possessee, stupid. Description, anything you think I should know about her."

"Oh, yes! Her name is Elizabeth Jordan. Address: 12 Vantage Street, apartment 2-B." He showed me a photograph. "Is that sufficient, Mr.... Mr....?"

"Call me 'Slimerod.' One more thing. Throw some money into this triangle for taxi fare. I don't like walking in winter."

I let myself in under the door. Two-B is a disgustingly tidy apartment. Not enough dirt anywhere to amount to anything. This broad obviously wastes a lot of time cleaning. Not like the magician's place. His home smelled like a public toilet.

Lizzie doesn't look like her photograph at all. For one thing, the photo shows her dressed. Here she is, sprawled out on the bed with nothing much covered by bare essentials, and I'm being charitable when I say that. Eve got expelled from the Garden of Eden for public indecency, and at the time, she was wearing twice as much as Liz. Bras hadn't even been invented then.

She is gabbing away on the phone when I enter the bedroom. I think humans are sensitive to my presence. Liz says:

"Stu! I feel a terrible chill ... like an icy fog rolling in across the room."

She should feel cold considering what she's wearing. Now this I can't understand at all. How come a nice-looking guy like my black magician has to fall for a dowdy dame like this? She's as homely as a bucket of worms. For one thing, her tits are too big ... no sex appeal at all. They wouldn't be so bad if they sagged or hung down to her waist like her hair. The waist itself is too small. Her hips and ass make up for it though. Liz must be what they refer to as a 38-28-37. Must be tough for a young broad to be deformed that way.

She's a brunette. It's also plain that she wastes a lot of time with a comb and brush. Give me the stringy-haired type any day. Her teeth are revoltingly regular and as white as pearls are supposed to be. Just my luck! On these jobs I never get any of the good-looking ones like ... Cinderella's step-mother.

I touch one of her ankles. Yech! How clean! I pull myself onto her. This is going to be an ordeal. Well, I've never failed ... got that reputation to uphold.

She yells into the telephone, "Stu! Help! Something touched me."

She continues to blabber into the phone. But not for long. It falls to the floor. The first step in possession, you understand, is you got to get inside. That's where all the controls are. Outside possession is rare. I've heard about it but never attempted it.

Entering is accomplished through any orifice. In women, most of the time it's through the mouth. That's because it's usually open. A lot of the guys prefer to use the nostrils or ears, but give me the mouth every time. Once inside, it takes a while to get oriented.

Every possession is different. I take over by short-circuiting various nerves, blood vessels, muscles, and body function controls. This usually takes hours. Don't believe what you've heard about some demon moving in and taking over right away, it's impossible. First of all, demons don't possess people. They torture and torment people, but they don't possess them. That's not a demon's job. If you know of any demon possessing anyone, let me know. When my union gets done, there won't be enough left of him to starch a collar. Sometimes, if the victim is exceptionally strong-willed, it takes days to dominate him.

I want every one of my appendages to be in just the right place. I didn't earn my reputation for meticulous craftsmanship for nothing. A lot of my fellow imps are slipshod and eventually get expelled, but not me. I work by the rule book; I'm an old hand. Lizzie screams.

I feel around and locate the scream control and suppress it. She can't talk or yell now. All she can do is gurgle and make meaningless noises. Lizzie drags herself off the bed and starts knocking things over. She smashes a vase into the vanity mirror. Just like a woman to start untidying at a time like this. I take over the muscles control. She falls to the floor and tries crawling. She gibbers into the phone.

A man's voice is coming out of the receiver; it sounds alarmed.

"Liz! Liz! What's the matter! Speak to me!"

Now to test my control. I make her roll over and pick up the phone. I force her to say, "Nothing! Nothing is wrong! I was just being playful."

The voice wasn't exactly right, but that'll come later. For the time being, I can pretend Liz has a cold. The excuse wasn't great, but it'll have to do on the spur of the moment. I can't lie off the top of my head like humans.

Okay, girl, now hang up. Damn! But she's hard to control. These modern broads are tough. Finally I bend her to my will, at least temporarily. She doesn't want to obey and still is fighting me. It takes a long time ... too long actually. If they get any tougher, I'd better start thinking about retiring.

Let's run through a few exercises to practice my control. First, jumping jacks. "Up, down! Up, down!" Now a few push-ups. "C'mon now, you can do better than that. Get those tits off the floor." These half-bras are more for looks than anything else. Later, when my control is absolute, she'll obey me as quickly as she would obey her own commands. "Now, we'll do a little jogging in place. Good! We're getting there. Enough for now. Let's go into the kitchen where you can pour me a nice refreshing glass of vinegar and Tabasco sauce. I sure earned it. Look at the time! Have I really be at it this long? Damn! The doorbell rings!"

Should I ignore it? No, it might be an important appointment, that might cause complications later. Better check it out. It rings again. Okay! Okay! Whoever you are, hold your horses. C'mon, broad, turn around and head for the door.

Hmm! Good! There's a one-way peephole in the top panel. Let's see who's outside. We look though the hole. There's a young, blond-headed guy standing in the hall. He's holding a black Gladstone bag. You can tell a doctor anywhere. Good thing I checked, those bastards can get stuffy about missing appointments. Let him in, Lizzie. We'll fake through the examination and send him on his way. I say 'fake' because I don't know what's wrong with her. I can make her do and say things, but I can't read her mind. Possession isn't that complete. Liz is aware of everything, but she can't do anything about it. She's a spectator in her own body, so to speak.

She opens the door and the doctor steps in. Ugly-looking specimen. Six feet four if an inch. Around two hundred pounds. Built along the classical Greek lines with finely flowing muscles and carefully chiseled features. Too symmetrically proportioned. Everyone knows the Greeks didn't know anything about masculine beauty, or feminine beauty for that matter. Blue eyes; strong, even white teeth. What a pig!

Instead of asking, 'Miss Sterns, how do you feel?' the guy comes over and gives her one of those long, lingering kisses. She returns it eagerly ... too eagerly. What a yechy feeling, my control slipped for a moment.

"Stu! Help me!"

I hadn't meant to let that get out, but, as I said, my control isn't perfect yet.

"What's wrong, Liz?"

I don't like his voice either, too manly. I force her to say, "Nothing, Stu, nothing! I had an accident. Help me clean up the bedroom like a good boy, will you?"

He looks at us ... that is, he looks at her strangely. Wish I knew exactly what was wrong with her. We wander into the bedroom. He looks at the wreckage.

"You must have had a dizzy spell, Liz," he says. "I'll have to give you an examination."

He sets the bag on an easy chair and removes his coat. "When did you begin having these spells, Liz?"

I make up an answer. "Early this morning."

"About what time?" he removes his tie and rolls up his sleeves as if getting ready for a barroom brawl. I wish I knew exactly what this examination is going to involve. I should have thought of something different.

"Eight o'clock," I respond.

"That's odd! I didn't leave till ten and you seemed perfectly well then."

Damn! I make her say, "I hid the symptoms. I didn't want to worry you." Which on second thought was pretty stupid. That's exactly the stuff you don't hide from a doctor.

"Very considerate, my dear. You didn't want to worry me while I was at Alvin's?"

"That's right. I knew you'd need all your wits about you. Is the dear fellow all right?"

Immediately I knew I'd said the wrong thing.

"He's fine. I certainly did need all my wits about me. Those birthday parties for seven-year-olds are harrowing experiences. He thanks you for the catcher's mitt and baseball hat and wants to know if next year you'll give him one of those life-sized inflatable dolls."

This Alvin must be some kid, I force a laugh and make her say, "I'll think about it."

At this time he's busy searching around in the bag. Finally he finds what he's looking for, a thermometer. Some doctor!

"I'm going to take your temperature, Liz. Please undress completely."

I get to undress for him to take our temperature. Exactly what kind of doctor is he? He confuses me. Her half-bra and string bikini drop to the floor. Wow! Can she move fast when she wants to!

"Sit in this chair, Liz. Make yourself comfortable, no unnecessary movement. If you have a temperature I don't want to drive it up." He slips the thermometer between our lips. "Relax now."

He presses his head to our forehead. "It's cool! That is strange with a fever."

Hey! Whose idea was this fever? "I said we ... I said I was dizzy ... what did I say?"

His hands slip under our breasts and strokes them gently. Unexpectedly, he kisses each nipple. I don't think I ever moved so fast. If I hadn't yanked my extensions back they

78

would have been snapped off when the nipples erected.

She moans. "Oh, Stu..."

The sensation was indescribably disgusting. Did he say he didn't want to drive her temperature up? My whole surface area crawled as if covered with flies.

He takes the thermometer out of our mouth and holds it up to the light. "Temperature below normal. I'll have to take your blood pressure."

He straps the sphygmomanometer onto our arm and inflates it. Then he places a stethoscope over the brachial artery and releases air from the bag. He knows that much about medicine anyway. Or does he? His free hand is busy between her thighs ... our thighs ... her ... Did that magician say Lizzie was a friend of this guy's? I hope so. I wouldn't let a casual acquaintance take these liberties.

Involuntarily her legs part and she starts to sigh, but I suppress that. I believe she's actually enjoying this. He looks worried.

"Your blood pressure is low also."

The black bag supplies him with an ophthalmoscope. He looks into our eyes.

"Hmm! Insensitive to light."

"I'm run-down, Stu," I force her to say.

"In that case, I recommend you don't compete in the women's semifinals at Berkley Field."

"All right, Stu, if you feel I shouldn't..." Another slip.

"Berkley Field is an airport," he says.

He places something that looks like a cardboard tongue depressor in our mouth. "You need hold this only a few seconds. Ah!" He pulls it out. The portion that had been in our mouth turned green. He looks at us.

"Just as I suspected. You're possessed, aren't you, Liz?"

I attempt a laugh. "Stu! I don't know what you're talking about. Maybe you're the one that's run-down."

He's making a circle around us with a coil of rope from the handbag. I recognize it for what it is—blessed hemp. I won't be able to make Liz step over that.

"Please! Let's not play games. The results of the tests are all backward. The readings should have been high. Obviously, Liz's functions are being suppressed."

The black bag is inexhaustible. He holds a ciborium in front of us. "You know what this is, of course?"

I nod grimly.

"Now, accursed demon, identify yourself in the Name of He who cast thy master into the dark regions."

I have no choice, but I can still protest. "Dammit! I'm not a demon. My name is Slimerod and I'm an imp of the tenth degree."

"Identify the magician who ordered you to possess this woman."

Here's where I'm a smoother operator than the average imp. I never ask my clients their names, so I can't betray them. I say, "I don't know, we were never formally introduced." I couldn't keep the smugness out of our voice.

"It doesn't matter." He's outlining a triangle on the carpet with more of the rope. He places a white candle on each point. The candles are mounted in low, wide candleholders to keep them from falling over. That bag must be as big inside as a football stadium.

When finished he turns back to us. "Slimerod, you are commanded to appear in visible form inside this triangle."

This is good for a laugh: no one has ever exorcised me, and I let him know it in no uncertain terms. He doesn't appear in the least discouraged.

He says, "Virgins are my specialty." I don't like his laugh. Wish there was another imp nearby so that I could call on him for help. Have him possess this cuckoo and make him take a nice flying leap through the window. A drop, two floors, to a nice concrete sidewalk will do him a lot of good.

This is undoubtedly that Stuart Falcon James my client warned me against. Funny I didn't think of that before. What is the shameless bastard doing? He's taking off his clothes and right in front of Liz. I can't make her modestly avert her eyes. In fact, she's getting excited. "Stop it!" I have to repress her. Shameless hussy!

James opens a large jar of some ointment and begins to rub it on himself. "Want to help me, Liz?" She starts forward, and again I have to suppress her. He coats his entire body.

He asks me, "Do you know what this is?"

"Protective cream of some sort, I suppose. When I get done with this broad, you'll need everything going for you, so don't use it all now." Here I'm doing a bit of bluffing. I can't do anything to anyone unless I'm ordered to. Maybe I can get my client to have me possess James as a return favor.

He looks pained. "Protective cream? That's like referring to a Rolls Royce as a scooter. This was given to me by Marchosias."

If James is a friend of Marchosias, I'd better tread carefully. Marchosias is a renegade demon who helps exorcists. The damn fool attended too many revival meetings and got religion. James reaches into the black bag again for a directory, a who's who of hell, and reads my genealogy.

"Slimerod? Possessing imp of the tenth power. Has never been expelled." He looks at me with respect. "Delights in human misery and agony."

"Well, we all have our little weaknesses." I try to sound modest.

James returns the directory to the bag. He withdraws a long rosary which he hangs around his neck. Damn! He's well equipped. It wouldn't surprise me to have him take a fully equipped altar and a choir out of it.

The nervy bastard steps right into the circle with us and there isn't a thing I can do about it. Each bead in the rosary is a pit from the fruit of an olive tree growing on the holiest mountain in Jerusalem. Liz stands up though I hadn't ordered her to.

He takes us ... her in his arms. Our ... their naked bodies press together and Liz is radiating waves of ecstasy. Disgusting! How immoral! We ... they kiss. Their hands and arms are busy performing far from esoteric motions.

"Oh, Stu, make me feel good again." My control has slipped to an even greater degree than I'd realized. I have to retreat to the area below her knees. I can't stand these revolting sensations she seems to enjoy. "Stu! My feet feel frozen."

"We'll have to warm them up. So that's where you went to, Slimerod."

I can't respond. I've lost dominance over her verbal functions ... among others.

"Slimerod, I'm going to carry Liz out of the circle and put her on the bed. You know what that means, don't you?"

Oh, how well I know! I can't respond, but he knows the answer to that one too.

"I know you can't leave this girl except through an opening, so I'm going to force you upward. When you feel you've had enough, depart and appear in the triangle in visible form."

Oh yeah? I'm tough. I can take anything he can dish out. This guy is a master of foreplay. James begins by doing things to her toes that I'd rather not describe. He caresses her ankles, and the action moves to the soles of her feet. Next up the legs to her knees. I'm being forced up, up, up. Liz is enjoying this, but I find it nauseating. Now I'm curled up in a ball below her navel and above her ... Please don't expect me to use that word. Mother and Father taught me never to use language like that.

Whatever! James has his finger in it and is manipulating it in a way that sends ripples of that disgusting rapture through her. They're exchanging French kisses. Oh! Those unsanitary degenerates! Liz is rolling to and fro, waves of anticipation engulf her.

"Stu! Give it to me! Give it to me!"

There's a horrible discharging sensation and I'm almost washed out of her by a torrent of escaping fluid. I've never experienced such torture. I'm still in control of her stomach though. Just wait till she tries to eat, I'll give her a century-sized bellyache.

"I think it's time for the rod treatment," he tells her.

She spreads herself to receive him. One hand eagerly guides the cylinder into her and I find myself moving up and down on top of it as he thrusts and withdraws. A deep lunge and my head smashes against her sternum. And again! And again! And again! And again! Liz is in heaven.

"Oh, Stu! Make it last, make it last!"

"I have good control," he says. "I can keep this up for hours."

Liz undoubtedly knows that from past experience whether he has good control or not. That was for my benefit. Bang! Bang! Bang! My head keeps striking against the top of her...! Oh my poor head!

He might be able to last for hours, but I can't. I'll have to attempt dominance from the outside. Her mouth is open and Liz is crooning like a contented baby. I escape and slip around to her shoulders. I'll try to possess her by inserting my filaments into her nostrils. It ain't as bad out here, but it's bad enough.

"Oh, Stu! You're as wonderful as ever. How delightful to feel you thrusting in and out of me!"

"My pleasure. You have the loveliest, creamiest sheath I've ever entered into. Do you know any magician who would want you possessed? Creatures like Slimerod do not work on their own initiative."

"Probably my cousin, George Carleton Aper. He plays around with that stuff."

"Does he bear you a grudge?"

"It's possible. He doesn't like anyone. A smelly, revolting little man with ugly features. He wanted to make love to me and I laughed at him."

"You shouldn't laugh at black magicians, they're very sensitive. The next time he approaches you, brush his face with a sprig of fresh dill and he'll forget his intentions."

"I'll get a few pounds of it right away."

At a time like this they gotta indulge in small talk.

"What is his address?"

"He lives in the Marigold Flats, apartment 4-F."

"What degree magician is he?"

And all this time, in! out! in! out!

"Neophyte probably. He hasn't been at it very long."

They climaxed in unison, which, I hear, is something only rarely accomplished. How lucky I am! Their orgasm sends me flying toward the ceiling. It is only by grabbing a handful of her hair that I save myself a nasty bump.

They're still coupled together. Some workman! He forgot to take his tool out of her. I'm glad he isn't a brain surgeon operating on me. Or did he forget? They're staring all over again.

Later, I have to endure a mutual shower and supper. Nothing I liked, it goes without saying. They're enjoying it, though.

"Liz, you're a wonderful cook. What a pleasure to make love to you. It's so rewarding in every way."

"I've got to keep my lovers strong, Stu. Is the ugly little worm out of me yet?"

Ugly little worm? Who the hell does she think she's talking about? Wait till I take over again.

"No. He hasn't appeared in the triangle. Slimerod is probably lurking outside ... very close to you. He can't speak through your mouth, otherwise we'd have been getting a blow-by-blow opinion of the exorcism."

"Stu, do you suppose we could reach some agreement with him? He could possess me and you can exorcise me on a regular basis."

Aarrrgh! Those disgusting animals.

"I don't think Slimerod would agree to it. First, he has no free will to agree to anything. He is absolutely at the command of whoever summons him until he either prevails or concedes defeat. His kind enjoy only misery and despair; the more profound the misery and despair, the more enjoyable to him. Their values are reversed. What is beautiful to us is ugly to them. What is enjoyable to us is unendurable to them. He has probably been taking a frightful pasting during this exorcism."

It's been a pretty harrowing experience all right, but I'll wear James down. He hasn't the stamina to continue like this much longer, no one has. I'll wait until they're asleep and then I'll enter her again and make her cut his throat with one of the steak knives.

"How about some more lovemaking and then a bit of sleep, Stu?"

"I'm entirely agreeable."

One thing about this James guy, he's easy to get along with. He slips the rosary over his head and places it around her neck. Damn! Now I'll never be able to get back in her. And with that Marchosias cream he smeared all over himself, I'll never be able to touch him either.

They're back in the sack. "Liz, have you ever thought of installing mirrors over your bed?"

She giggles, the shameless bitch. "Often, I'd like to put them on the walls too."

What's he doing? Her legs are open ... as usual. What's he looking for down there? Oh no! He's not...! He is...! The utter...! Complete...! Pig!!!

I can't take any more. He'll be able to do that all week. "Hey, James! Knock it off! I concede! I quit!" I barely make it to the triangle. Once in it, I almost fall on my face. "I give up! Look! I'm in the triangle!" I'm screaming my head off at them, but they ignore me. Of course part of that is because they can't hear me. I gotta be hooked into someone's vocal system before I can make myself heard. I jump up and down and make faces at them, and they continue to ignore me.

Eventually they stop what they're doing and come over. Their arms are wrapped around each other. He tries to be cute.

"What did you want? A better view?"

"No! You indecent bastard!" I yell. "I give up! You win!" I have to write this in the air with a piece of colored chalk.

"He looks like a big dandelion spore, Stu. How is it that we can see him now?"

"The triangle is the only place you'll be able to. It's necessary so he can receive orders."

My chalk is flying. "C'mon now," I beg. "No more! I'm a prisoner of war and entitled to humanitarian treatment. All I'm supposed to tell you is my name, rank, and serial number."

He ignores that. "Did George Carleton Aper send you?"

"As I told you, I don't know his name."

"He's about so tall." Liz holds up a hand to indicate height. "Very pale face with lots of blackheads and a sunken chest. Bad breath."

"That sounds like him," I admit grudgingly.

James holds the ciborium in front of me. "In the name of the Holy Eucharist, do as I demand of you." There's no mistaking this guy's confidence.

"What choice have I got?"

"Return to he who sent you and fulfill upon him the instructions he intended for this woman. Aper lives at..."

"I know the address."

I forgot to ask James for cab fare. It's a long, bitterly cold walk back. Once, I get run over by a taxi, and once, a priest jogs over me. Naturally they can't see me. I'm visible to humans only in the triangle.

This assignment has been an unlucky one from the beginning. Finally I reach Aper's address and drag myself up four flights of stairs. I got to rest on each landing to catch my breath. I'm worn out. Maybe I ought to retire or find another job. But, at my age...

I slide in under the door. Aper is sitting in a chair staring into space. One thing, his apartment is a lot more livable than Liz's. I search until I find a piece of chalk and draw a big triangle enclosing both of us. Now he can see me. His mouth drops open.

"What ... what are you doing here?"

"I got exorcised," I explain grimly.

He looks astonished. "Well, I'll be..." Here he uses a four-letter word in the past tense indicating a degree of carnal knowledge.

"Not yet." I grab one of his ankles and drag myself upward. "But you soon will be."

The Perfect Beauty

excerpted from *The Silver Prince*

Gary Bowen

Brilliant uniforms of many colors moved through the streets, the foot soldiers trotting in formation, plasma rifles slung over their shoulders, while armored units tramped like elephants, tents quivering as they passed. I looked overhead, but the sky was clear, no subtle shimmer betrayed the presence of an active shield. Was it turned on? Were we even going to need it? Or would it be over without a shot being fired? Through the throng a lady approached, paper parasol painted with peonies shading her delicate Perfect Beauty mask. Orange-lacquered hairpins held the elaborate coiffure in place. She wore a leaf green cotton robe printed all over with a pattern of willow leaves, orange linings showing at her cuffs and hem and exuding a floral perfume. She wore straw sandals, and had a long knife thrust through her orange blossom sash. She started to kneel before me and I said, "Not here, not in the dirt. Please come in."

Obediently she followed me with little mincing steps: being a lady she wore a long robe without the free-moving divided skirt worn by active men. Her sash was tied in a huge formal half bow in back, and though she was tall for a lady, she reminded me of nothing so much as the porcelain dolls sold in duty-free shops throughout the universe. In the center of my camp, I turned to face her and she dropped to her knees, bowing all the way to the ground.

What was I supposed to do with her? Me, an old soldier accustomed to the hijinks of barracks sex, where you were likely as not to be surprised by whipcream-wielding clones or other pranksters. Sex among the Peacekeepers was about as decorous as chowtime—which was to say, not very. When you worked all day, you ate heartily and played hard whenever you got the chance. But now, here among the Shen, things were very different, and Garathan, my reason for being here, was gone. Grief squeezed my heart tight.

"Lady Willow, I presume." I found my camp stool and sank down on it, trying to arrange my dull black robe with modesty, if not dignity. I still hadn't gotten the hang of my new wardrobe—or new position, for that matter. The change from Peacekeeper grunt to *keppi* Death Priest for the Shen was a drastic one, though I wasn't sure that I had changed inside.

She straightened up and produced an orange fan from her sash, waving it back and forth while she nodded. Her gesture was a calculated one, and I wondered if "Lady" was a professional title. With the Perfect Beauty mask covering the entirety of her face, I had no idea what she looked like, or what thoughts were going through her head as she regarded the uncouth barbarian *keppi* Death Priest. Prince Garathan must have looked hard to get any takers for the position. Or maybe he'd pulled rank, pointed at somebody, and said, "You, you've volunteered." In which case she wouldn't be any happier about being here than I was about having her.

"I'm not entirely sure what's expected of a lady in your position. What do you do?"

Her small bosom heaved, and she spoke very softly, her voice distorted by the mask. She was not so calm inside as she was pretending to be. "My purpose is to please you, Lord."

"I'm afraid the things that would please me most are impossible for you," I replied sadly.

She crept a little closer. "I might surprise you, Night Lord."

"I have never been with a Shen lady; I am certain you would astonish me. However, I am not interested in surprises. I am too worried about someone dear to me."

"Tell me?"

The lady could serve one very useful purpose: she could listen sympathetically. I rose from my seat.

"Come with me, please."

I offered her my hand and lifted her to her feet, her orange blossom perfume wafting about me in a heady cloud. She made no demurrer as I led her to my tent. I paused at the door, looking around my camp, where the servants were all pretending to be intensely interested in their chores, sighed, and opened the flap to admit her. I tied the door tightly closed, for I did not want them to know what I wasn't going to do with the lady. I sat down on my pallet, and she knelt before me.

"Tell me what troubles you, my lord," she crooned to me. "And I will do what I can to set it right."

It was a tempting lullaby, one that gave my heart a little ease, even though I knew her concern was dictated by her profession and not any knowledge of me and my needs.

I took a pale green paper out of my sleeve and unfolded it, showing the flowing calligraphy to her.

Beloved, for some time I have pondered the requirements of your Rank, and I have come to the conclusion that it is best for you to take a concubine suitable to your Office, while carrying out your duties as best as you may, trusting in Divine Providence to provide a suitable solution to the dynastic difficulties. Accordingly, I have selected a lady of some quality, whom I hope you will receive favorably.

Now that peace has been concluded with the Pangu, and the Barren Lands are preserved from harm I have resolved to present myself to the General of the Eastern Gate, bowing my head to whatever judgment may fall upon me. It may well be my doom to die by my own hand, but I shall die at peace, knowing that I have done all a man and prince might do for the preservation of his nation.

Garathan.

It was sealed with the moon and crescent seal of the Silver Prince.

"I want him back! I don't care about politics, or dynasties, or anything else! He doesn't have to die!" I crumpled the paper. "The Shen are idiots who can't accept defeat, even when they are overrun, and who would punish the one man who has been able to salvage something of the situation. They expect the impossible."

"But that is the way it is, and it is better to submit with dignity than to become a fugitive upon the road, welcome nowhere, in danger all minutes of the day and night."

"I don't care! I would do anything to be with him!"

"Anything?" she asked.

A nimbus of pale light radiated from the woman, and I saw then that she was not some floozy bought in the marketplace, but a messenger of the spirits. The destiny of the moment weighed heavily upon me, and I knew that whatever I asked would be granted—if only I would pay the price. I closed my eyes and thought, but all I knew was that no matter how unjust the spirits' dominion over men, yet still they could grant my heart's desire. I knew then what my answer would be, and understood at last how easily the unseen Powers ruled the Shen.

"Anything," I whispered.

"Would you go into exile with him? Take the road as an outlaw or beggar, fleeing before the Golden Wrath, you and your beloved marked for death at the hands of any who might discover your identities?"

"Yes!"

She removed her mask.

"Garathan!"

"I love you, Brice. I will give up my Rank, my Office, my Blood, and my manhood, if you will have me."

"Yes!" I pulled him to me, crushing his lips with kisses, and forcing my tongue between his teeth. He let me, his body passive under my hands. I didn't care; all I knew was that he was mine, all mine, finally without reservation.

"Is this a wig?" I asked, touching his hair.

"No, it's mine. You wouldn't believe how long it took to have it done either."

I took hold of the two large clips decorated with flowers and pearls. "And if I pull these it will all come undone?"

"Yes, but if you do—" I pulled, and waves of black hair cascaded down. "—I won't be able to put it back," he finished.

I laughed. "I don't care." Then my arms went around his back and unraveled the bow. I unwound the lengths of brilliant fabric, opening the layers of his clothing, exposing his hard young chest. I noticed he had changed the old bar jewelry for silver rings, and I sucked one into my mouth, tugging it. He cried and arched his back, so I nibbled the pierced flesh, making him arch and cry some more. My fingers clenched in his sleeves, holding on tight enough to make my knuckles turn white. I flicked the nipple with my tongue, back and forth, back and forth, while he panted. "Oh, Brice," he moaned. "Oh, Brice, I have no shame."

I pushed him down onto his back, and lay on top of him, pinning him beneath my weight. I bit his earlobe and he pressed his cheek against my mouth. With one hand I tweaked his nipple, and he grew hot, sweat dampening his collar. When I pinched his nipple, his back arched and he cried out, but I was not so green as to think I had hurt him. I pinched him again, and he jerked again, crying louder. I shifted lower, kisses trailing down his throat, pausing to suckle each of his nipples, while he lifted his hips and rubbed his hot flesh against me. I kissed his belly, tongue dipping into his belly button, and pulled away the lengths of fabric twisted about his legs, revealing his hard-on. We had to pause a moment to disentangle him from the cumbersome clothes, and then he lay naked before me, black hair disordered against the quilt, long legs flexing restlessly.

"Do with me as you will, Brice. I am no longer a Prince and I live only to serve you."

"Anything?"

"No taboos," he breathed.

I parted his legs and he cried out, even though I had not hurt him: he was afraid of what he had promised. I didn't want him to be afraid; I wanted it to be the best thing that had ever happened to him. I lay between his legs, kissing his thighs, working back and forth between them while his hands clawed the quilts. When I reached the apex, I pushed his knees up to his chest. He cried out again, but I kissed him right in the middle of his ass. He grabbed his legs and held them while my tongue explored each wrinkled detail of his asshole. He let out a series of sharp cries, legs jerking, ass muscles twitching under my touch, so I kept licking and kissing his narrow flesh. He wailed in frustration, and a low rumble of thunder echoed him.

"What do you know?" I said raising my head. "It might finally rain."

"I don't care! Fuck me!"

I kept eating his ass while with my other hand I fished through my dopp kit until I found a tube of lubricant. I closed my mouth over his cock as I slid my finger into him, and he hyperventilated, his body caught between my mouth and my hand. I massaged the inside of his ass, loosening the tight sphincter, and letting him get used to the feel of it. Then I added more lube and a second finger, gently massaging his prostrate gland and resisting the urge to simply stick my cock in him and fuck him senseless.

"I'm going to come!" he cried. More thunder rumbled outside, and the tent sides billowed before the rising wind.

I grinned at him. "That is the idea."

But I didn't want him to come quite yet, so I repositioned myself. "Ready?" I asked him.

He nodded violently. I slid into the sweetest place I'd ever been, and he locked his ankles behind my neck, hanging on for dear life. I braced myself on my hands and began a slow steady stroking, while his hands grasped the edges of my open robe and pulled hard. "Oh, Brice! Yes! No! I don't know what I want!"

I laughed, then, maneuvering carefully, rolled onto my back, bringing him with me so that he landed on top of me without us coming apart. He looked surprised. I tucked my hands behind my head. "Enjoy yourself. Do whatever you like. Have fun!"

"I have to do it?" He was blushing.

I grinned and nodded.

He braced his hands against the mattress, lifted himself carefully, then slid down. He twisted a bit, his eyes rolling as he discovered the different sensations he could create for himself. He moved more surely then, finding the most effective rhythm for his pleasure, sliding up and down my shaft, taking it exactly as deep and fast as he wanted it. His face contorted as he approached his climax, and he sat down hard, driving me deep into his flesh. Then his hands grasped his jutting cock and started pumping. I nodded encouragement.

He stroked himself with long hard motions, panting for breath, oblivious to the sound of rain on the roof of the tent. His groans drowned out the growl of distant thunder, and I let myself drift, enjoying the way the noise of the drumming rain drowned out the sounds of the world preparing to go to war, heat flooding through my body as I felt his passion building.

A sudden cold drip right in the middle of my chest made my eyes fly open, and another drop joined the first. I bit back a curse because Garathan was close, and I didn't want him to lose it. A third drop of water hit me, then a fourth and a fifth. Garathan let loose a long low animal cry, his eyes clenched tightly shut, all his muscles flexing as his hot semen splattered on my stomach. Then I didn't care about the rain; I bucked beneath his weight, ramming myself inside him, hands clenched on his thighs, until my cock throbbed with pleasure, and I stopped breathing momentarily.

Garathan held up his hands in surprise as he finally noticed the leaking roof, and said, "Rain." Then he looked at his hands and looked at me. "Rain! Brice, rain! The First Sign, the Potency of Life! Rain!"

I remembered him showing me the First Sign an aeon ago: kneeling in the sand, hands uplifted, face tipped up: same pose as now. "Wonderful, but I'm getting wet!"

He got up and we pulled the bedclothes out of the way. The rain seemed content with a single leak, and I was glad it wasn't worse. Water trickled across the reed mats that floored the tent and ran under the wall and into the yard. I poked my head out briefly, and saw that the Black servants were battening down the camp, while soggy banners snapped in the wind, and trash blew past, carried aloft by the rising gale. Garathan poked his head out too, then grinned at me and withdrew. I closed the flap again.

"Do you see? Ton Shen does not have to be barren any longer. We can make it rain!"

"You think so?"

"Sex magic," he stated emphatically. "It doesn't have to be a man and a woman to make it work." Then he drew my face close to his and kissed me thoroughly. "I should learn that when I am afraid, it is best to be brave and keep going. Because when I do, marvelous things happen."

I smiled happily at him, glad to see he had finally come to terms with his desires. "Going into exile won't be so bad. We can go offworld. I'll get a job as a security guard or some such thing, and you—well, I'm sure the Federal Intelligence Agency would be happy to hand you a sinecure."

He picked up the orange fan and snapped it open and closed. "I'm not going offworld, Brice."

"Why not? We can't stay here, for chrissake!"

"Don't swear at me in your vulgar tongue. You know I am a Prince of the Blood, and I can't leave here."

"Hey, what happened to us running away together?"

He lifted harrowed eyes to mine. "I understood something just now."

I sat up in alarm. "What?"

He shook out his long warrior's hair and braided up his queue. "I was born to rule, Brice, and by the Moon, I will!"

"Emperor?" I asked tentatively, wondering if I was finally catching onto dynastic politics.

He hesitated. "I can't claim the Gold as long as my mother lives; that decision is made by the spirits. But I can be a Silver Emperor. That color is mine by rights; no one can argue it."

"Like the Silver Emperor that founded Hu Shen?"

"Exactly. I shall announce the rebirth of Ton Shen and make my capital here on the site of the old capital: Ton Far."

"It's a worthless hunk of desert. Holy doesn't pay the rent, Garathan."

He smiled. "We know how to make it rain, don't we? And there's platinum here, and quicksilver. It's enough to buy both the Peacekeepers and the Pangu to fight against the Eastern Gate."

"Civil war."

"If I gather a large enough show of force they'll have to come to terms." A silver light radiated from his naked skin, and his Power crackled around him. The spirits were on his side; how could he fail?

Further debate was futile: all that remained were the details.

The Arrows of Devotion

Thomas S. Roche

Lurette stood before her cauldron, a study in carved ivory: impassive. In the boiling cauldron she could see the battle outside. The bloodshed, the terror, the mutilation—it was familiar to her, unfortunately, for she lived in an empire torn by strife.

Lurette could hear the familiar battle cry of the Imperial Guard, could see the flash of the bright knives as they corrupted the flesh of the rebels. She took a handful of scented powder from the bowl beside the cauldron, and sprinkled it across the scene. With a sizzle, wisps of sandalwood-scented smoke arose from the cauldron. When the scene faded into the black liquid, she turned to Yves and considered his face, which remained as impassive as hers. The sandalwood smoke caressed his flesh.

Yves knelt in chains, his wrists bound with cast-iron manacles behind him, his ankles held far apart and fastened to posts so that he could not stand—in fact, could hardly move. Lurette walked over and stood before him.

"I'm really quite sorry," she said. "It's the law. Empress's order. Do you truly hate me? Tell me the truth, now."

"No," said Yves solemnly. "I understand your obligations, Mistress."

Lurette's cold, white hand slowly drifted up Yves's body, her fingertips encircling his very pointed chin, lifting it up so that his beautiful obsidian eyes were elevated toward her. In solemn deference to her authority, he kept his eyes down. Lurette's painted thumbnail pressed against his lips, parting them. His tongue grazed the tip of her thumb.

Lurette spoke very softly, as if she knew the answer already.

"Yves, if I were to unbind you—"

Yves turned his head forcefully away from his mistress, tearing free. He looked at the ground.

"Mistress," Yves snarled arrogantly, suddenly agitated, squirming in his bonds. "Don't ask me that."

Lurette's white brow furrowed. She bent lower, bringing her face very close to his. She reached around, sliding her fingers into the cascade of black hair that tumbled down his back.

Lurette gripped hard, pulling Yves's head back, forcing him to look at her. Both of them knew that his arrogance would have cost him dearly with any other mistress.

"I'm asking," said Lurette. "You know my feelings on male freedom. Now tell me the truth."

Yves remained silent.

Lurette caressed Yves's face with her fingertips. "You make things so difficult for me. You know my views, and you know how they have caused me no end of suffering, and nearly brought ruin upon my house. You know what I would do if the law were mine to change. I have even told you how I would repeal the amendments. I have suffered for your kind, to give you some rights. Now, Yves, I ask for something very simple:

tell me the truth. Tell me what would happen if I were to unbind you."

The sound of breaking glass filled the parlor. The cauldron had flared to life unbidden. Lurette lifted her hand. She heard male screams far below. The sorceress waved, and the firelight from the cauldron disappeared again.

Yves raised his eyes, staring defiantly up at his mistress.

He spoke firmly, slowly.

"If you were to unbind me," said Yves, "I would be forced to join the struggle of my brothers."

Lurette considered that for a moment.

"This I know. But what would you do to me?"

"That," said Yves, "I would rather not think about."

"Truth," said Lurette. "Give me the truth. Suppose you were free, in this room, holding a blade, and I were unarmed. For that matter, imagine that I were bound. What, then, would you do?"

Yves laughed. Lurette's back straightened: she had never heard a man laugh before. They were not allowed to do so in the presence of a woman. It sounded ... odd, somehow ridiculous—harmless, irrelevant, unlike a woman's laugh. But somehow appealing, just the same.

Lurette released Yves's hair and face and stalked across the room, her boots clicking on the stone floor as she looked out the broken window. There were fires in the distance.

"I would set you free, Mistress."

Now it was Lurette's turn to laugh. "I asked for the truth, Yves. You must give it to me."

"I assure you, Mistress. Were you to emancipate me, I would join the struggle. I would fight for the freedom, for the separatism of men everywhere. I would fight and die if necessary to bring this freedom about. But at the same time, quite in conflict with my obligations to my brothers, I would fight to protect you. Even though it should bring me the contempt of my compatriots." Yves hesitated. "I truly believe that you, unlike so many, are a decent woman."

Lurette felt a warmth go through her body. She returned to Yves, standing over him, enjoying the feeling of strength.

"Touching," she said. "But is it true?"

"Of course," said Yves bitterly. "But there's no way for you to find out for sure, is there?"

Lurette's eyes had misted, and a teardrop fell on her slave's upturned face. The teardrop rolled onto his lips and he licked it, savoring the salt taste of his mistress's agony.

"Yves, I have fought in the Council for the freedom of all men. I have tried to enact legislation to prevent this bloody uprising. You remember the Land Equalization Act ... I have even backed the pro-male lobbying groups, such as they exist. You know all of this. My secret, though, the secret I'll now reveal to you, is that I cannot live without you. You bastard, you've stolen my heart. And thus I cannot entirely devote myself to your cause."

Lurette moved closer, pressing Yves's face to her stomach. Obediently, touched by her devotion, Yves began to kiss her bare belly, savoring the feel of the jeweled ring against his tongue. He let his tongue snake into the subtle depression, tasting the salt of her sweat. The nights had been hot lately.

Lurette's eyes were now filled with tears, and she began to weep as Yves's tongue drew circles on the smooth flesh of her stomach. "For this devotion, I beg forgiveness." Lurette sighed. "And now I've another confession to make.

"On the outskirts of the city, there is a cache of weapons. In the catacombs which lead out to the wilds. Certain of my compatriots are women of somewhat lower stature than myself, who feel that change must be made, by force if necessary. They are waiting in the catacombs with enough weapons to ensure the establishment of a male settlement. I have already obtained agreements from the partisan leaders that escape will be their objective—escape alone, not revenge."

Lurette smiled: "You know the leader of the partisans?"

Yves's back stiffened. His tongue stopped its probings in Lurette's navel.

"Of course not, Mistress. I do not associate with revolutionaries..."

"Don't be a fool," spat Lurette. "I asked you a question. Never mind," she said. "You know him. He is your brother Justin. I do not entirely trust this man, perhaps in part because I know his brother too well."

Yves was beginning to understand.

"My soldiers await my order. Those arms will be delivered to your brother's partisans only if I can secure a suitable hostage, to ensure that Justin's sentiments toward revenge do not change in midflight. A suitable ... and willing hostage.

"So you see, Yves, I offer you a choice. I cannot live without you. But I will set you free. You can join the fight, gain your freedom, though that fight may be doomed and the freedom short-lived." Lurette had begun to weep again, caressing Yves's face.

"Mistress ... please do not—" began Yves.

She cut him short. "Your other option is eternal devotion to me, with the knowledge that your brother and his partisans have escaped the yoke of the Empress. But that devotion, devotion to your mistress, must be eternal."

"It would in all cases be eternal, Mistress. My devotion to you..."

Lurette shook her head. "That devotion will be *eternal*. Complete. Unwavering. Absolute."

"I don't understand you, Mistress..."

"Do you agree?"

Yves's eyes clouded over. He shut them, his mind alive with visions and possibilities. His breathing became short; his head began to ache. He saw himself running in the grassy fields to the west, where he'd been taken once but, of course, not allowed to roam. He saw himself free, set free upon the winds like a falcon, never again to wear the collar, never to answer another's questions with a meek voice. To be his own man, to become what he would.

But there were enormous dangers in freedom. Without the arms that Lurette offered, the partisans would surely die. But they would die free men: on their feet, not their knees. Yves felt a stirring of pride as he imagined his sacrifice, cut down by the Imperial Guard while he stormed the castle with a thousand of his fellow patriots, bearing sharpened sticks and rocks.

The option, for Yves, was an eternal and luxurious submission at the feet of his booted mistress. This was a life with which he was already very familiar. Yves knew intimately the sweet taste of his mistress's body, the ivory curves and subtle textures of her physique. He knew the pains and the pleasures of her dominance. He knew the kindness of her generosity and the cruelty of her lash. He knew well the flare of her anger and the fury of her punishment. And he knew she did not dole out that punishment often, nor lightly. Yves understood, deep in his soul, that Lurette was a much sweeter mistress than nature, or freedom. Her taste was saffron and her scent rose petals. Her flesh was ivory. Only her claws were iron.

Yves pressed his cheek against Lurette's white belly.

"I agree," he said. "In exchange for your assisting the partisans, I will remain with you. I offer you my eternal devotion, Mistress."

Lurette's body shook slightly. She put her hands into Yves's hair, pulling him tightly against her stomach. She wept as he began to kiss her, offering his submission. Lurette brushed wet black hair out of her face and licked her lips, hiding a shudder of relief.

Her voice was clear and resonant. It did not betray the surging emotion underneath. "You must understand that that devotion is immutable. It will be assured, and cannot be withdrawn. You will live and die in your devotion to me."

Yves spoke softly. "I understand, Mistress. My submission is immutable. Unchanging."

Lurette had finally subdued her tears. She pulled away from Yves and stalked across the room, her white legs flashing in the moonlight.

Lurette rang for her guards. The door creaked open. Under martial law, she was obligated to keep Yves fully manacled except in the presence of at least two of her female servants.

The two women appeared in the door to Lurette's chambers. Lurette admitted them. Lissa and Caliva were her personal guard. Both were trained to perfection, their naked bodies taut, powerful machines of bone and muscle and sinew. Their heads and bodies were shaved, and the nipples of their slight breasts were pierced with posts. The two guards were nude except for their battle gear: bracers of metal, leather sword-belts, knee-high leather boots that buckled in front and laced up the back and came to sharp metal points at the tips of their toes. Their flesh was oiled for battle. Each woman bore a tattoo on her belly: Lurette's device.

Lurette greeted the women and solemnly issued their instructions.

"Yves is to be pierced tonight. Place him on the platform in the second dungeon. And ensure he is well bound and hooded. Caliva: you will perform the piercing."

Yves's face had gone white. In his years as Lurette's slave, he had never been pierced. Now, upon offering Lurette his complete submission, Yves would finally give up control of his body. His eyes were wide as he looked up at Mistress Lurette, begging leniency. Lurette stood over him, caressing his face.

"I'm sorry, Yves. I trust you completely. But I ... in order to give the order, I must be assured of your total submission. I will ask her to make it quick."

Lurette's boots echoed down the hall as she left the room. The two servants came for Yves. He closed his eyes as their arms circled him.

Yves was taken, wrists bound, to the second dungeon. The first dungeon was where he had received his brand, a legal requirement for all slaves of the Empire. That had been several years ago. It seemed like an eternity that he had been on his knees before Lurette.

Yves was forced to his knees so that he could be collared and hooded. Lissa stood before Yves and pressed his face against her. The flesh of her belly was warm, and smelled of sweat. Lissa tied back Yves's long black hair while Caliva, standing behind him, slipped a thick leather collar around his neck. He felt the collar being padlocked.

Lissa finished with Yves's hair. Caliva handed her a leather hood. Yves drew a sharp breath while Lissa hooded him. He felt the well-oiled leather surrounding his face, enveloping him completely. Only the mouth was open, allowing him to breathe. The leather of the hood was more supple than glove leather but still quite heavy. The hood fastened with a series of laces down the rear, and a collar that buckled just under his chin. The two collars fastened together with a second lock. Caliva began lacing the hood slowly up the back of Yves's head, pulling the laces tight so that Yves was quite aware of each aspect of his bondage. Caliva chuckled when she was finished. Lissa tested the security of the hood and the collar with her ivory fingertips. Yves breathed slow and deep.

Yves had become erect, as the law required of him. But the two guards did not put him to work, since Lurette had not given them permission to do so while they secured him.

The two guards bound Yves to a platform in the middle of the room. The platform was designed of wood, roughly cut in the shape of a man. His head was cushioned in a gentle "U" of silk, but held in place by the leather collar around his neck, which was fastened by a lock to the neck-piece of the platform. His arms were bound firmly, the cool iron of the manacles encircling his wrists. His legs were similarly spread, held by iron. Heavy leather belts went around Yves's belly and thighs. His naked body was opened, exposed, displayed for Lurette's review and possession. He could hardly move.

Locked deep inside his own kind of darkness, Yves felt a hand slowly creeping up the inside of his thigh. He quivered slightly in his restraints.

Lurette's voice was clear, a whisper in his hooded ears. "You are my only prized possession, Yves. I would gladly give up the riches of my office, if only I could keep you in absolute submission. But that submission must truly be absolute."

Yves felt cold fingertips encircling him. He was being measured.

"You will be pierced in the places that signify complete submission. But you will not be pierced by steel, or by silver, or by gold. You will be pierced by quite another metal, if you agree to it.

"You know well my powers as a sorceress, Yves. I have been conducting a clandestine search. My retainers have finally discovered the mine which many women thought was only legend. Some say it is the place where the Goddess of love first obtained the metal to make her arrow-tips. She has, ever since, been piercing the hearts of mortals with those arrows and causing no end of mischief." Lurette sighed, pausing to kiss Yves on his leather-clad forehead. "She pierced my heart deeper than any, as I laid eyes on you.

"Of course, these stories might be nothing more than legend. We are going to find out, you and me."

Yves felt the head of his organ being positioned. Caliva was ready to initiate the procedure.

"You must now make your decision, Yves. I will allow you to renege on your agreement, and thus I will set you free. But if you say my name, now, I will order Caliva to continue."

Yves's throat was tight. He squirmed slightly in his bonds, but of course his body was fully immobile. He thought of the fate of his brothers if he did not submit to Lurette, if she did not supply the weapons they so badly needed. He imagined his own body prostrate before the Mistress. There could be no turning back, under the powers of her sorcery.

Softly, he spoke his mistress's name.

Lurette did not reply. Yves senses were alive as he felt Caliva gripping his organ.

"Breathe slowly," said Caliva. "In, out. In, out. Counts of four."

Then, with the agony of a thousand screams, Yves felt the needle being forced into his body.

The bonds prevented Yves from moving as she pierced him. The agony of the needle being drawn slowly through was more than he could bear. He tried to scream, but of course it was only a muffled sound inside the hood.

Once the needle was through and the ring had been placed through the tip of his cock, Yves could feel the static charge of the magic inside him. Welling up in his hard organ as if ready to explode. But the hood covered his eyes, prevented him from completing the spell. The ache of the magic inside him was more painful than the piercing.

Lurette had seated herself across the room, watching silently as the procedure was performed. The warmth of arousal coursed through her.

Yves's nipples were placed in tiny clamps. The pain was, again, terrifying, but the needles went through quicker. His back arched as she inserted the two rings. The charge of sorcery was more than he could stand. Yves began moaning. His entire nude body was on fire with the power of the uncompleted spell. His soul was alive with the need to complete the enchantment. To open his eyes and behold the object of his devotion.

Lurette was a skilled sorceress. She had hooded him to build the tension, to allow the magic to rise to its highest potential before she discharged it into Yves's supple, vulnerable body. And the hood prevented any untoward mishaps. He could not accidentally lay eyes on Lissa or Caliva. Yves would remain in the state of undischarged magic until Lurette chose to release him therefrom.

Yves would have been in pain even without the magic. But the sorcerous metal was like a burning force coursing through his naked body, running hot from his loins to his nipples and back again, a triangle of unending torment. Yves felt Lurette's hand encircling his member—how well he knew the touch of her fingers, how intimately he knew the sharp edge of each of her fingernails. She squeezed firmly. Yves moaned, low in his throat.

"Take him to my chambers," said Lurette. "Bind him to the bed, and leave his collar and hood. Carry him gently." She released her grip on Yves's manhood.

"Your bed, Mistress?" It was Lissa who spoke.

"Yes," Lurette spat imperiously. "My bed. On his back."

Yves dimly felt his wrists and ankles being unfastened, the straps around his thighs and waist being swiftly unbuckled. He was lifted by Lissa and Caliva, carried out of the dungeon and up the stairs. The power coursing through him caused his mind to dim, his vision to catch fire with stars, his pulse to race. He felt as if, at any moment, he could explode. Raging within him was the desperate need for total fulfillment, for enlightenment, for devotion. But the need was without object. It was maddening.

Yves was laid face-up on Lurette's soft feathered bed, the caress of the silken blankets encompassing him. His limbs were stretched expertly by Caliva and Lissa, until he was spread-eagled. Yves felt the restraints being buckled around his wrists and ankles. The two guards fastened his limbs securely to the four corners of the four-poster bed. Yves was once again immobile. The smell of Lurette's bed was overwhelming. It was the smell of incense, of sandalwood, of dried rose petals and musk, of Lurette's sensuous body, her sweat, her sex. He heard the guards fumbling with the bed's curtains, drawing them shut so that Yves was in total isolation. The silence enveloped him.

He inhaled deeply of his mistress's scent: sweat and perfume, roses and nightmares. He felt the power increasing in his body, aching for release.

It was a very long time before Lurette entered the bedroom, accompanied by Lissa and Caliva. The two guards stood beside the bed and drew back the curtains for their mistress. Yves felt the soft touch of Lurette's hand on his belly. Her hand felt unsure, awkward, blind. But at his mistress's touch Yves's flesh quivered. Yves was a writhing animal, unable to control the energies which flowed through him. Lurette knew he would die soon if she did not release him, allow him to look upon her. But the longer she waited, before the critical moment, the more complete his devotion would be when he finally opened his eyes to look upon his mistress's face and body. And Lurette had no intention of letting that critical moment pass. She had no intention of allowing the slightest harm to come to Yves.

"I'm sorry to have kept you waiting," said Lurette breathlessly, hardly able to contain herself. "I had ... some business to attend to."

Lissa or Caliva—Yves couldn't tell who—took a moment to light the two candles within the canopy. They would bring the much-needed light inside, and were scented with jasmine.

Yves moaned softly as Lurette undressed with the assistance of her guards. They unbuckled her leather boots and breeches and placed them near the bed. Lurette slid, like an angel, onto the bed, her naked body brushing Yves's at a thousand places. Her cool skin enveloped him.

Lissa and Caliva pulled the black velvet curtains shut, then tied them securely. The two guards left the room, to stand their watch immediately outside the door.

Lurette hovered above the bound slave. She sensed the power she had over Yves, almost painful to wield. Lurette knew the height of the sorcerous metal's power had arrived. She reached under Yves's head. As she unlaced the mask, she spoke softly.

"Listen carefully to me, Yves. Your eyes are about to behold the fairest sight they will ever rest upon. Before they do, know that you will never belong to another. I am your final mistress."

Lurette unbuckled the collar just under Yves's chin.

Lurette uttered a silent prayer for forgiveness, to some dark goddess to whom she had not prayed in years.

Her fingers were shaking. Nervously, Lurette removed her lover's hood.

Yves's eyes were darkened, unfocused from hours under the leather mask. He was only dimly aware that his mistress, too, wore a leather mask, one that buckled securely behind her head, and that she was deftly working the buckles with her fingertips.

Yves shut his eyes, his mind overwhelmed. Slowly, he let his eyelids flutter open as Lurette finished removing her own mask.

Lurette's red lips parted slightly, a little cry escaping them. Faintly, Lurette began to moan. She forced herself to stop, wrestling control back into her body. Lurette remained frozen, staring down at Yves. Her face became a mask of impassive strength. But her black eyes were filled with tears.

It took a moment longer for Yves's vision to clear completely. Lurette's face, emotionless, impassive, burned itself into his consciousness as it formed above him. He would always remember the face without emotion, its black eyes glistening wet.

Lurette rose on Yves's body, her thighs spread around his belly. She displayed her body for Yves to understand, and know, the creature that owned him. She was power, rage, hatred, love, an impassive goddess of danger and need.

The tears broke inside her eyes. One rolled down Lurette's cheek and fell on Yves.

Yves's eyes flickered over the naked angel atop him, over her muscled shoulders, her slender throat, the cascading black hair that scattered about her upper body. He looked upon her flat belly with its ornamental piercing, the flare of her hips, the powerful vise of her thighs spread around him. His eyes lingered over the swell of Lurette's breasts, and the thick rings pierced freshly through her nipples. He understood in a moment what had occurred, while he writhed in desperate need on his mistress's bed.

"Oh, Mistress," he whispered.

Lurette began to laugh, low and cruel, the laugh turning into a delighted, hungry moan.

With vicious condemnation, she hurled herself upon Yves.

Lurette sank her teeth into the flesh of his shoulder; she let her fingers stray over his face. She caressed his black hair, losing herself in its silken texture. She rubbed her naked body against his, her passion rising as she moved her way up and settled down atop him again, hair streaming over her to scatter on his chest. She placed each of her pierced nipples in his mouth, allowing Yves to taste his mistress's blood. Lurette crawled on top of Yves's head and lowered her spread thighs onto Yves's face. With desperate need and full devotion he began to service her. His tongue found its way deep inside her and Lurette cried out many times as she writhed over her slave.

Yves knew, as he pleasured his owner, that the taste and smell and feel of his mistress would implant themselves on his tongue and nose and skin in the same way her appearance had implanted itself on his eyes. He would never be free of her, would never forget. She was his last, and only, Mistress. The arrows of devotion had pierced his soul, and his eyes were opened.

It was some time before Lurette sprawled, spent, alongside Yves. She had long ago unfastened his wrist and ankles, for there would never be a need for physical restraint again.

She coiled her naked body around Yves, her ivory fingers moving gently across his belly.

"The order has been given, Yves. I was true to my end of the bargain. As you were to yours. Men shall be free, in the wilds. But never in this bed."

Lurette's fingers spread slowly around the tender flesh of her nipple, acutely aware of the pain in the fresh piercing. The ornamental piercing in her navel, too, had been replaced.

"It is too much," wept Lurette softly. "Too much happiness, to be pierced, both of us, with the arrows of devotion..."

She circled Yves with her arms. Lurette whispered her silent prayer, once more, knowing that she was forgiven. Outside, it was dawn, but the bed remained in darkness.

Dragon's Fire

Jack Dickson

I stared at the last glowing embers of the camp fire, then raised my eyes to the dark sky. "Want to hear a story?"

Johnny shifted in my lap. "I've heard all your stories, man..."

Looking down, I tried to smile. "Not this one. It's a story about the past ... and the future ... and maybe even the present." I felt him shiver in the cool night air and move back against my chest. "Interested?" I reached forward, nervously poking the dying coals with a stick.

He stretched languidly, catlike, making himself comfortable between my thighs. "Okay, then ... I'm listening."

As twin moons slipped into their descent, I began my tale.

Breathing broke the humid silence: the shallow, easy breath of sleep, and the troubled, erratic inhalations of the sleepless.

Saja edged Ver's arm from around his naked waist and sat up. Sweat pinpricked his brow. He frowned: nights had been hotter than days, recently—a sign? He flicked the tent's door-flap aside and gazed out into the night.

Soon, there would be only night.

Eyes acclimatizing to the velvety pitch, Saja stared into the distance, beyond the Fini encampment to the great cimma forest ... or what remained of it. Where once had stood majestic rows of tall, proud trees stretching up into a lilac sky...

Saja focused on the sparse clumps of decaying wood, rotted by the slow but certain climactic change. He turned away from the wasteland, glanced back into the tent.

Ver was snoring gently, pupils flitting beneath eyelids.

Saja smiled and continued to watch as Ver's chest rose and fell with an oblivious rhythm. The smile slid into a frown.

Ritual ... the ritual of Fire.

Dragon's Fire.

Breath caught in his throat. Old Yrad's ravaged face flashed into his mind. Saja looked up into a dark purple heaven and cursed.

Fire Gods ... dragons...

The Old Ways.

He shrugged off a shiver. Change ... everything ran its course. As nomads, no one knew that more surely than the Fini. Saja thrust a hand through thick black hair in frustration and scowled. Circumstances changed ... change was part of life. Adaptation was the key to survival, and the Fini knew all about adapting. The tribe had survived near-extinction before, and would again...

He peered beyond the night sky into distant galaxies twinkling with life and a myriad opportunities.

What would happen?

What did the future hold for Ver and himself? What was the best he could hope for?

An icy hand gripped at his soul.

The Ritual of Fire would go ahead; Yrad and the Old Ways would be proved right; he would live to a ripe old age...

Torrents of cold sweat poured from his forehead, running into his eyes and mixing with the salt tears already forming there. Saja released the tent flap and moved over to Ver's sleeping form. Maneuvering them both into their familiar S-position, he molded himself around the golden figure and buried his face in Ver's shoulder.

Saja would live to be a ripe old age, but would be alone forever.

I felt Johnny's blond head resting heavily against my chest. "You still awake?"

"Mmm..."

I smiled, wrapped my arms around him. "Want me to go on?"

Another sleepy, monosyllabic response.

I sighed and continued.

Yrad bowed, made the sign of Vala, then raised cataract-clouded eyes. From his knees he stared at the seventy-seven onyx steps which led to the altar. He watched the unending procession of Fini slaves as a cargo of precious cimma wood made its way to the very top. His heart swelled in his chest. At last his tribe would have a home, Esidarap would be forced to accept his people's right to be there. For millennia his ancestors had traversed galaxies like so much rootless seed, settling wherever the wind blew—and then for only as long as their hosts would permit.

Generations of Fini had attempted to settle in many lands, tried to adapt, to fit into their environment. The Old Ways had been abandoned, the Great Book and its teachings consigned to a select few, passed down through the generations until the knowledge and the faith, the belief in the Fire Gods resided in Yrad, and Yrad alone. Until now...

He stared beyond the line of industrious workers to the fading rays of Esidarap's sun.

This planet was dying. No amount of thought or action on the part of Esidarap's native intelligentsia could change that.

But he could change it. When the Great Day came, all would be forced to admit that the Old Ways were best.

Yrad stared at the icon, at this moment under construction by three sweating, uncomplaining slaves. Pride overwhelmed him. His heart leapt as he gave thanks to the ancient Fire Gods, who had not deserted his people in their hour of need. Through their auspices, he had received insight into young Ver's great gift, a gift that promised redemption, rebirth. A gift to replace the dying corona which was gradually fading to nothingness above Esidarap's sand-covered surface. The Fini shaman edged to his feet, stretched out his gnarled arms, and began the morning prayer of supplication. "Oh, Vala...!"

The workers ceased laboring, fell to their knees.

"...thanks be to thee for guidance! Thanks be to thee for wisdom! Thanks be to thee for knowledge in our ignorance, sight in our blindness, light in our darkness. Soon, as it is written in the Great Book, Ver and Ukiro will join under your benevolent gaze. The union will be fruitful: the fruit of Ver's loins is fire, a fire which has raged unabated for one thousand cycles..."

Yrad closed his rheumy eyes, voice soaring up through the atmosphere.

"...he bears the mark of the Dragon. Dragon's Fire beats in his heart, flows in his veins. Bless this union. Give us a son!"

⚘

"Swords and sorcery!" I heard a sleepy but familiar skepticism in Johnny's voice. "I don't believe in all that rubbish." Suddenly sly. "You know the type of stories I like..."

Nuzzling his neck, I made him silent. "Shh. Listen. Listen and learn."

⚘

Saja smiled, watching as Ver braced his arms against the rock and submitted to the scraping. Copper skin glowed under the helion's weakening rays, shining from both the oil and the sweat which poured from the hard body. Saja pressed the ivex scraper firmly against the muscles of Ver's back, which arched reflexively. As he ran the ceremonial instrument down over the arcing incline and onto tightening buttocks, a sigh escaped Ver's lips. The sinewy body convulsed as tiny droplets of cimma oil leaked into the deep crevice between two hard mounds and trickled down the inside of one thigh.

Saja raised the scraper, running a rough finger over the dull edge where Ver's sweat and the sacred oil had collected. An aroma drifted up, filling his nostrils, his heart and his mind, as he wanted Ver to fill his body.

It was not to be.

A groan from the rock beside him dragged Saja's mind back to his duties: the Preparation.

The Preparation for Fire.

Ver was the Chosen One.

Saja shivered as the shaman's ancient phrase crept into his brain.

As the eldest son of the Fini tribe, Ver's candidature had been assured from birth. Lineage and legend had proclaimed his eligibility...

Saja lowered his eyes to groin level.

...the sacred mark confirmed it.

The Fini had rejoiced. A Chosen One: after centuries of waiting, of wandering, the honor had fallen to one of their own. Esidarap's survival was in their hands ... or rather, Ver's loins.

Saja pulled his thoughts away from the inevitable and laid the slick ivex scraper on a rock ledge. He began to massage Ver's sweating shoulders with expert hands.

The groans deepened as his strong fingers kneaded the hard muscle, rubbing away the tension, the apprehension, the fear.

Saja reached over and kissed the back of a moist neck, enjoying the texture, the saltiness on his lips.

His lover's skin.

His brother's skin.

Under his hands, Ver twisted unexpectedly and turned to face him. Saja paused, gazing into the eyes of the one who, regardless of his destiny, formed and filled his world. But the bright, auric pupils spoke another, less welcome message: *The mark of the Dragon makes me special ... the mark of the Dragon occurs only once in three thousand years ... the Dragon is not for you.*

Saja smiled while his soul leaked the tears of a thousand and one empty nights. He watched as Ver blinked, lashes sparkling a little under the sun's faint rays, the returned the smile.

They stood together under a lightening lilac sky until Saja lowered his eyes and took a step back, almost ashamed. Ver's body always overwhelmed him. He winced as an arrow of jealousy pierced his heart, then turned away.

He knew he was a disappointment to his family—to the entire Fini tribe. It was only through Ver's insistence that Saja was allowed to even associate with the Dragon, let alone steward the Chosen One. Stocky where Ver was tall, heavily muscled where Ver possessed the streamlined sinews of a swimmer or runner, hirsute where Ver's golden body had been virtually hairless even before the shaving rituals had begun, ebony-eyed and raven-haired where Ver's blond, golden-irised characteristics were classically Fini. Saja's dark eyes darkened further with black memories.

Children of his own and other tribes had teased him at school, calling him Vini—a pun on the Esidarapian word for "dark horse"—whereas *Fini,* according to the Great Book's ancient dialect, translated as "golden warrior."

Saja clenched his fists, as he had clenched them for years, never allowing the taunts to hurt or affect him; never complaining, never retaliating. After all, they were right—weren't they? He was an anachronism, a throwback to a more primitive era—maybe even a prank played by the mischievous Fire Gods, who, legends told, were often eager to swap their own children for a Fini cherub.

Strong arms reached under his shoulders.

Saja leaned back into another sweating body, feeling the hardening buds of Ver's nipples crushed against the tufted skin around his spine.

He didn't care if he was different, not really. Ver was with him; he was with Ver—they had loved each other as long as either could remember.

As children: with a child's unquestioning, unconditional love.

As youths: with youth's curious, physical love.

As young adults: with an ever-increasing emotional love.

And now, as grown men, with all the trust and respect which sprang from a mature love: a love which acknowledged all previous loves, combining and creating a love which was more than the sum of its parts, a love which burned in their hearts with the passion of fire.

Dragon's Fire.

Then slick arms languidly turned him around, pulling him against a smooth, gleaming chest.

Jack Dickson

Saja sank into the embrace, pressing himself into his brother's firm flesh, loving the feel of his own rough, matted pectorals on Ver's smooth sinew. Resting his head on a well-covered collarbone, he instinctively began to rub himself up and down Ver's naked thigh as he felt hands travel down from shoulders. Fingers lingered on his waist, toying with the hide thong which held the traditional steward's uniform in place. Saja tensed as a hard index finger worked its way beneath the leather strip, lifting the well-filled pouch until the loose flesh within was as tight and constricted as the sun-dried leather encasing it.

He gasped into his brother's shoulder, pressing open mouth to warm flesh, hands lowering themselves down past Ver's waist, settling on two hard mounds of muscle. The pressure in his groin increased as he continued to undulate.

He bit his bottom lip, feeling Ver release the thong, then lower both hands. Fingers spread over hard buttocks.

Saja moved onto his toes, allowing access, then raised his arms to Ver's neck and massaged with his thumbs as his brother's thumbs hooked up toward the very heart of him. The leather pouch was held in place by the swelling of his passion, its thong torn away by Ver's eager fingers. Eyelids closed, Saja raised his head and felt Ver's teeth nibble the skin of his neck. He was thrusting urgently now, moaning with pleasure as a thumb pressed against the tight ring of muscle, seeking entry to his hot body. Inside, another circle recognized the digit, spasmed in welcome as the first wrapped itself around Ver's thumb in a pulling motion. Saja clenched his teeth as a nail's, then a knuckle's, length entered him.

Ver's arm was around his waist, holding him tightly as the slick thumb edged back, then thrust harder, deeper into his body, slowly at first ... then more vigorously.

Saja felt his breath quicken, become more shallow as Ver continued to thrust. Tension began to mount; wild thoughts

120

flashed through his mind as Ver pressed skin to skin ... thoughts of Ver's thumb, fingers, tongue ... thoughts of his own body deep in Ver's sweet mouth, the feel of Ver's lips and teeth along the length of him.

His mind was reeling back and forward across the years, across the memories, across all he and Ver had been to each other, of the perfect union, of his own body deep inside Ver's as his brother's thumb was now deep inside his...

As the weakened sun of Esidarap neared its apex in the purple sky above, another, stronger son of Fini neared a pinnacle of his own, on his own. Hips shuddered, thought dissolving as his body dissolved. Saja thrust forward against his brother's thigh as hot waves of milky liquid drenched the ceremonial pouch, leaking out onto hotter flesh. Lights danced on his eyelids as Ver's four fingers pressed against his buttocks, holding the thumb in place, forcing it ever deeper as muscle spasmed and sparkled like a thousand shooting stars.

Through the shattering orgasm, Saja was aware of the rapid beating of his heart, of another heart's slow, steady beat ... and of the dragon which lay sleeping against his own thigh.

"What's his problem?" Johnny sounded more alert now—this was the kind of story he liked to hear.

"Whose problem?"

"The Ver guy. Why's he not hard?" A hand played along the inside of my thigh. "I mean, if it was me, and some hunky guy was..."

"Shh!" I smiled, knowing I had caught him, drawn him into my story. "I know patience isn't one of your virtues..."

Ukiro wandered around the encampment, eyes drinking in familiar sights, sights she had grown up with. She wanted to see them as if for the first time, wanted to imprinted the minutiae of everyday life on her retinae, wanted to take this world with her when she entered the next.

To be selected to receive the Dragon was a great honor, Ukiro knew that. She glanced over to the tent where her life partner, Micha, and their three daughters sat, grooming. So why did she not feel honored? Why did she feel like hiding, fleeing, crying, screaming with rage at the honor that was to make her name last forever in the hallowed halls of Esidarap's history?

Ver opened his eyes, focusing gold pupils on the eight inches of lifeless flesh which lay between his legs. He blinked through the gloom. Each day since puberty he had come to this cave—in the beginning to enjoy its restful qualities, the tranquility it somehow instilled into his racing mind and pulsating body. When he was younger he had come here of his own free will, but under the tutelage of Yrad, the visits had become routinized, part of his instruction, his induction.

Reaching down, Ver pulled back the hood of skin and stared at the small white circle just below the head of his thick penis. He inhaled slowly.

All this—years of control, of learning to understand his body, understand its special qualities, the role this bundle of sinew and veins would play in all their fates—because of something which looked like a flaw, an imperfection.

Ver traced the pale circle with a smooth index finger. The heavy organ, tamed by meditation, twitched almost imperceptibly under his touch. He inhaled deeply, redirecting the frisson of pleasure which shot up his spine, held the breath, then exhaled.

It was Saja who had first noticed the mark of the Dragon. Ver's penis jerked again at the memory: a night, almost a decade ago, lying naked on the warm black sand under a glowing moon, his brother's full mouth nuzzling ... then stopping:

"Oh...!"

Concern in the rich, dark voice as Ver had gazed down past Saja's glossy head to a faint, vaguely circular outline on the underside of the rod of hardening flesh.

He almost laughed out loud, remembering their panic, remembering the frantic washings, the cimma infusions, the guilt ... culminating in his first, timid visit to Yrad. Ver sobered, recalling the look of disbelief, then awe that had crept across the ancient shaman's face. He closed his eyes, index fingers absently rubbing the sacred mark, remembering how he had sat cross-legged with Yrad on this very spot, listening with growing anticipation to the Elder's words of explanation:

"There is nothing to fear, my child—you have done nothing wrong. On the contrary, you have been blessed with a wondrous gift. What lies in your loins is something of great beauty and strength, of immense wonder and spiritual power. You must not abuse that power, but learn to control it, hone and develop it, because, one day, the future of those whom you love—the very survival of us all—will depend on you."

In the darkness of the cave, Ver inhaled slowly. The sense of pride and responsibility was heavy, tinged as it now was with more than a little fear. Ten years earlier he had listened to the venerable sage's words, answering the strange questions with tremulous nods and shakes of his blond head. Yes, he had already received pleasure from his body: Yrad didn't seem surprised. Yes, he had become aware of a strange heat in his loins at the moment of orgasm: Yrad had nodded, enigmatically.

The first lie had come easily: no, he had never lain with another. Yrad had smiled, resting a craggy hand on Ver's shaking shoulder. "That is good, my child—that is how it should be. The ways of ordinary men are not for you. Your destiny is as a high priest of Fini, and as such your body is

123

sacred. It holds the Dragon, the Fire Dragon, and the divine breath of the Dragon. Now that the sacred mark has appeared you must guard the Dragon and its fire."

Ver opened his eyes, inhaled the damp, slightly musky odor of the cave's interior. He had tried to keep faithful to the oaths he had sworn to the shaman ten years earlier. The tantric vows had not been broken. He had not spilt his seed since the sacred mark's appearance. Not by his own hand, not with man, nor beast of the field.

Ver shifted slightly on the uneven, rocky floor. A warm glow spread over his body as Saja pushed into his mind. Countless purple days and nights—in their tent, under the stars, by the running water of moonlit streams. The feel of Saja's hot skin on his, the taste of Saja's sweat, the texture of hard lips, of rough dark stubble against his own hairless face, the weight of Saja's tongue twining with his own...

The fire inside increased. Ver tried to clear his mind.

...the thickness, the smell of his brother's glossy hair, the pressure of Saja's knees in his armpits, the heaviness of Saja's strong form as Ver took his brother into his mouth, caressing him with lips, edging tongue under the loose sheath of darker skin, even nibbling that darker skin...

In his loins, the sleeping Dragon moved against a sweating thigh.

...and when Saja was moaning and thrusting deep into his soft mouth, when Ver had licked and sucked so that the hard organ pressed against the back of his throat with unbearable urgency, he would gently ease himself away and then stare ... just lie and stare up at his brother's glistening, shining member as it stretched almost vertically from the impossible tight root...

Ver became aware that his breath was losing rhythm, was coming in short, shallow pants. He knew Yrad would not be pleased, but he also knew he could control the Dragon, control the fire which burned deep inside his body, as he had controlled it for years.

...they moved well together, so well that the progression was super-fluid, two sides of a mirrored reflection. Saja would roll from astride him, clasping tightly and taking Ver with him, until Ver was on top, squatting over the gleaming, saliva-soaked rod. Entwining the slick fingers of one hand with his brother's, Ver would reach down and guide that member, pulling down and back until the shining, exposed head leant against the quivering entrance to his own body. Then he would pause, as he always did, pause and look down into dark, bottomless eyes. Ver received great joy from the pleasure he gave to Saja; joy by proxy, as they both knew, but any physical discomfort was eclipsed by the expression on Saja's face as Ver lowered himself, impaled himself, thighs trembling, onto the thick staff of flesh...

Ver cried out, so great was the desire and longing. Naked, and still shining from the cimma oil, his torso shuddering with sobs, he stretched his arms upward toward the roof of the cave. In his mind's eye his fingertips gouged through the stone and up into the clear night, wanting to pluck down a star, maybe a surplus sun from some distant solar system, and deliver it to Yrad—deliver what Esidarap lacked by mortal means—rather than suffer this curse.

I felt the tension in Johnny's hard body.

"That's not ... fair!"

"What's not fair? That Ver's never experienced..."

"You know damn well, Ian." He moved from my lap and settled a few yards away. "That stuff about the white patch ... on Ver's..." Johnny's eyes avoided mine as he refused to finish the sentence.

I held out my arms. "Hey, come on! It's only a..."

Johnny turned away, ignoring the gesture.

I stared at the back of his blond head while he toyed with the fire's dying embers. "I didn't mean to..."

"Just get on with it." His tone was harsh.

Doubting for the first time the intention of my tale, I found my mouth was dry.

Standing before the sacred altar as the last few lengths of cimma wood were positioned, Yrad felt a fluttering deep in his ancient chest.

A sign?

He gazed up into a hazy purple sky. The sun seemed to weaken before his eyes, flickering dully through cataracts.

A sign?

The Gods of Fire spoke to him as his heart rhythm altered, stuttered, then began again. Tingles played up and down his right arm, stiffening and relaxing in turns.

A sign.

A sign.

Yrad fell to his knees, left arm clutching right as the beating in his chest echoed in his ears. He opened his mouth.

Silence.

Yrad evoked the shaman voice of a thousand generations of Fini shamans. Captured by the breeze, the unspoken command was carried on the wind to all corners of Esidarap.

The Fini heard it.

...laboring in the fields, they heard it.

...planting in the forests, they heard it.

...talking in tents, they heard it.

In her life partner's arms, Ukiro felt the command, and her heart died.

As a body, the entire Fini tribe stopped what they were doing and began the journey—whether short, whether long—toward the altar.

All except two. For the power of the Fire Gods holds jurisdiction over only two elements: earth and air.

Ver loved to swim with Saja. He loved the feel of cold, clear water pouring over his face and hair. He loved its fluidity, its restrictive inertia. He loved to battle against the fullness and weight of it. He loved the way it cooled his body, deadened his mind of worry and distractions until only one thought remained. In the mountain stream, he opened his eyes as his body broke the surface skin and looked around.

No one.

Nothing. Only rock and sand and scrub land...

A splash beside him. Ver grinned as strong arms seized his waist, pulling him back down into the icy depths.

In the clear water, Ver tried to catch his brother off-balance, wrestle him to the riverbed. But Saja was too quick for him. Powerful legs were around his waist, squeezing tightly, and Ver found himself on his back, on the smooth floor of the river, lungs bursting.

Then Saja's mouth was open on his, breathing into him, into his chest, his heart, filling Ver with something other than air. Between almost-numb thighs, the sleeping Dragon began to stir.

Gasping, they shot toward the surface.

Head once more in the keen air, Ver watched his brother shake himself like a dog, scattering droplets of spray in a wide arc. Something rang in his mind, the echo of a thought. Ver smiled, shook it away like his brother shook the water from his brawny body. Glancing down, he saw the length of Saja's love for him, the measure of desire projecting up from a wiry jet forest. Ten years of restraint ebbed away, ten years of denied response, ten years of unfulfillment, of ... selflessness.

Saja was with him always. Even in the cave, Saja was increasingly there, in his mind, when that mind should be on other, more important matters.

But what was more important than life and love?

What was the basis of life?

What—who—was the nadir and apex of his own life?

For a second, Ver considered Yrad, his family and tribe. Then he thought of Ukiro, of someone he had never met but whose life he would end.

A life for a life, a son for a sun.

What was life without love?

The sleeping Dragon began to uncurl.

Recklessly, selfishly, Ver pulled Saja to him, felt the hard heat of another body close to his, shadowing the solar heat which pulsed in his veins.

The sleeping Dragon was stretching to full length after a decade of slumber.

He laid a hand behind his brother's neck and raised the powerful face upward, leaning into a kiss. Saja's mouth was urgent, his tongue a familiar explorer. Ver felt strength course through his body, mixing with the fire, tempering heat with other heat. Instinctively, as Saja had done on many occasions, Ver began to undulate.

The Dragon twitched its tail.

Open-eyed and open-mouthed, they communicated without words, with pleasure, with joy, with their bodies.

Ver gasped as the Dragon reared, then hissed. He felt his brother pause in the kiss, slowly edge away and look down to where a tiny white pearl brushed the Dragon's mouth.

The fire was pulsating now, the heat of a million fires focused into one man-made, man-oriented inferno. Ver felt his scalp tingle with a thousand tiny sparks.

He tilted Saja's face to his own. His brother's expression was one of confusion, wonder. Ver laughed, as he had not laughed in a decade. It was time for laughter, for seizing the moment. Both knew the risks. Both knew the price.

Grabbing his brother's outstretched hands, Ver led him though the cool water and onto the riverbank.

"No!"

Johnny now sat close to me, my affront forgotten as he was drawn into the story. He clutched at my arm. "He's a priest! He can't! What about the planet and the ... Old Ways? It's not right. They're being ... selfish."

"Who's selfish?"

Johnny scowled. "Ver and the hairy guy. They're only thinking of themselves and..."

"Ver and Saja are in love, Johnny. Each is thinking of the other, not himself."

"Yeah? What's Yrad gonna say when he finds out?"

Reaching down, I hooked my hands under his arms and heaved him up over my body. He fitted against me eagerly, easily. "You mentioned a sacrifice—there are many types of sacrifice..."

In the arms of a burly slave, Yrad allowed himself to be carried to the foot of the altar, where Ukiro, pale and trembling in a white ceremonial loincloth, stood waiting. Through eyes misted by the pain in his arm and chest, he watched the beautiful maiden cast a pain-drenched look to her life partner and daughters, who stood yards away at the front of the swelling crowd. Above, the sun was fading fast. Shadows lengthened around the altar, dragging the seventy-seven onyx steps up into infinity. Night was falling.

A sob from Ukiro split the silence.

Barely able to speak, Yrad tried to reassure her in whispers. "Do not be afraid, my child. It will be quick, and full of joy. Ver has guarded the Fire Dragon well. There will be no pain, no regrets, nothing ... only life."

Stroking the blond head, I looked into the night sky. The two moons were almost gone and on the horizon a pinkish glow was appearing.

Muffled words breathed onto my chest hair. "Poor Ukiro. Does this story have a happy ending? It's gotta."

I sighed. "Happy for whom? Happy for..."

He nuzzled my hardening nipple. "Don't stop. I need to know."

Naked, the cool water rapidly drying on his hot skin, Saja stared at the golden Dragon, and the proud head licking upward from a bush of saffron hair. Breath caught in his throat as the fire-beast swayed under his gaze, brushing his brother's navel, edging up the bronze stomach until it stood completely erect.

Ver's hands were warm on his waist.

Saja flinched. Jumbled emotions rushed through his mind: guilt, lust, fear... He looked back up at Ver's handsome face, the face he had known since childhood, the face which had for the past decade been clouded with worry, with tension, with the strain of enormous responsibility. Now that face seemed younger and older at the same time. Ver's eyes were glowing, the yellow irises alive with fire.

Ver looked happy.

Slowly, Saja reached out a hand, brushing the burning face with his knuckles, then stretched down and stroked the Dragon's back.

I pulled Johnny's head closer to mine, until I could feel the beating of his heart, feel his breath on my shoulder, his lips warm against my skin. We began to move.

Darkness shrouded the planet. Ukiro's tread was heavy as she mounted the onyx steps, heavy as her heart, heavier than the tears which sparkled in her brown eyes and coursed down over a silken cheek.

Yrad watched her slow progress, watched while pain shivered up and down his arm. Doubt glistened at the edges of his mind as his eyes flicked between the solitary figure on the onyx steps and the weeping Micha. He pushed doubt away.

It had to be.

The Fire Gods had spoken.

Ver must have a female partner.

Ukiro bore that honor.

The Old Ways.

The Old Ways were best ... best ... best...

I rolled Johnny over in the cool, black sand, enjoying the feel of his body against mine, his hardness against mine.

"Don't stop, man, go on."

Story or movement? I didn't know. Was it really important anymore? But I wanted to start what I had finished, though the pink horizon grew to a golden red. I eased myself up, and nestled Johnny between my thighs. One arm around his waist, I pointed into the sky.

As the Dragon pulsed in his brother's shaking hand, coalescence exploded in Ver's brain.

Yrad had been right.

This power ... a fierce, a power beyond anything he had ever experienced. Tongues of flame spoke to him, their voices deep in his soul as his whole body focused first into the Dragon, then spread outward toward Saja.

Fireworks filled his eyes. Saja gasped in the darkness as Ver's body began to throb with a light that seared his vision, singed his flesh, and burned into the very heart of him. This was life; this was love; this was past, present, and future, regardless of anything Yrad had ever said, regardless of the destiny of a civilization or the future of a world. He felt selfish, achingly selfish.

And selfish felt right.

With no regrets, Saja moved forward and pressed himself against a pillar of flame. A hot mouth was open on his. Scorching breath filled his lungs, choking, cauterizing.

Then he felt his brother's hands on his shoulders, lowing them both to the ground.

On the seventy-seventh step Ukiro paused, stared over at the cimma marriage bed, at her funeral pyre. Silence rang a death knell in her ears. Below, the crowd was swelling. She couldn't look down, dared not look at the face of her life partner and the children they had mothered together. Instead, she raised eyes heavenward, into the purple darkness.

In the distance...

I waited and watched.

"You're a real tease, you know that, Ian?" Johnny wrestled free from my grip, spun around to face me. His legs astride my waist, his hazel eyes searched mine.

"I'm only the storyteller. I..."

132

"Well? Come on, man!"

The Dragon was breathing fire, now. Burning lava filled his body as Ver stared deep into ecstasy-filled eyes. With Saja's strong legs over shoulders, he pushed down, pinning his brother's body to the ground.

Straining muscles stood out on Saja's thighs as Ver maneuvered the Dragon toward the pulsating entrance to his brother's body.

The Dragon inhaled, then breathed out.

Ten years of longing slipped away as the Dragon sank into Saja's body. Ver felt strong muscle accept, then close around the Dragon, caressing, harnessing ten years of his own passion and the power of the ancient Fire Gods. Pressing his mouth hard to Saja's, Ver thrust deeply, toward his brother's soul.

Amidst a shiny, auric halo the golden warrior and the dark horse were united by the Dragon.

I moved my gaze down from Johnny's dilated pupils. Behind us, the glow threw our shadows together onto darker sand. His hands reached out for mine, found them. Fingers entwined, and we stretched our arms toward the lightening purple sky.

Yrad blinked. At the periphery of his vision, something sparkled.

Breath filled the air. The crowd inhaled as one.

Where there had been only darkness, a golden pinprick...

Johnny was staring over my shoulder. Transfixed as I was by the golden skin of his face, my words soared like birds into the dawn sky.

Two became one, seared into a molten mass of burning flesh. As Saja's tongue flicked the inside of his mouth, Ver gripped his brother's slick waist with fire-tipped fingers and felt the Dragon throb. Gold irises stared into dark, liquid pools as Ver's body merged with Saja's. Physically, they had been one many times. But not like this.

Riding the Dragon.

They were burning, alight with life, love, and fire. White heat soldered limb to limb, legs, arms, hands, eyes.

No Ver, no Saja, no Dragon, nothing but heat and fire and love.

Insolation filled them as the blaze increased. Far from taming the Dragon, Saja's body pushed up the temperature, ignited the already blazing union, drove it forward, degree by degree.

"Yes, yes, yes..." Johnny's breathy voice filled the morning air.

Ukiro's eyes felt rather than saw the star widen, grow in the purple heaven. Shadow vanished as a thousand flares exploded in the sky, bringing life where there had been death, heat where there had been chill.

Light, where there had been darkness.

Heat warmed the back of my neck as twin suns rose over the horizon and the lack sand sparkled with life.

As the molten mass of Vala coursed from his soul and up into his brother's body, a rush of burning air propelled Ver upward, into and away from Saja at the same time. Through scorched golden irises he could see his brother's joy, feel it as a palpable presence, feel it intensify as the Dragon's breath poured into Saja's body, sealing them together in a bond of pure energy. They were together ... together forever in...

Johnny was on his feet, pulling me upright. "Look!" He raised my hand toward the horizon. "It's Saja and Ver! It worked, didn't it?" He turned the face of a happy child toward me. "They did it—they had a son—two suns, really!"

I smiled, staring down between his naked thighs. "Love ... and magic, Johnny—the magic of Ver's very difference." I ran a gentle finger over the patch of discolored skin which had caused him to pull away from me in shame.

Johnny flinched, then relaxed. "I know, man, I..."

Then his mouth was on mine, his sweet mouth moving with mine as we kissed under our planet's twin suns. The heat we generated almost—but not quite—matched that of Ver and Saja ... and we didn't need to die to stay together.

He pulled away first, breathless under the fire of our kiss. "Hey! What about poor old Yrad—what happened to him?"

I laughed, draping an arm around his broad shoulder. "The Esidarapian paramedics reached him in time, and he lived in Paradise to be four hundred and two!"

Johnny squealed with delight. "Oh, man ... you and your stories!"

We picked up our clothes and began to dress.

Fleeing Gods

Mary Anne Mohanraj

Helena struggled out of sleep, blinking her eyes hazily against the darkened room. It had been a most vivid dream. Since she'd left her spineless husband and the regular supply of dull sex, she'd often had erotic dreams. Somehow none had been quite this ... explicit. A tongue had licked her instep, her toes. Teeth had nibbled on her calves. She had almost been able to feel the muscled body, the sensuous hands caressing her thighs, her hips. She could almost hear his heavy panting, and smell his strong breath.

Actually, she could still smell that strong breath, that unmistakable mixture of strong spirits and poor oral hygiene. There was a strong scent of aroused male in the room. Helena suddenly sat up and switched on her halogen lamp, ready to grab it and crack it on the skull of any would-be rapist.

As the light flooded the room, an immense man reared up on the bed and away from her, raising a hairy arm to block his eyes from the light.

"Shut that off, wench! You'll ruin the mood!"

Wench? What kind of man calls a woman wench? Helena relaxed a little, still retaining her firm grip on the lamp, and peered at the impressive stranger in her bedroom.

"What are you doing here?" she asked him, quite calmly, she thought.

"Seducing you!" he thundered. "What does it look like I'm doing?" He lowered his arm a bit, piercing blue eyes blinking in the light like those of a dazed deer. Helena stared intently at him, hungrily drinking in the obvious strength in those arms, that chest. The man was positively bristling with hair, and muscles bulged under the thick brown coat. Something else bulged too, an enormous penis that stood out proudly from his naked body. Helena had been married for seven years, and bar-hopping for three, but she had never seen anything to match this before. She licked her lips.

He blinked at her, looking a little confused. Then he seemed to gather himself together. He started shouting again.

"Fear not, fair maiden. I am the greatest of lovers, renowned in seven kingdoms and across seventy seas. No harm will come to thee!"

Helena winced at the volume. "Could you lower your voice a little?" she asked, as she started to shift her body, preparatory to sitting up. The man immediately flung himself down on her, pinning her to the bed. Helena just lay there, enjoying the weight of his body on hers, the teasing scritch of curly chest hair against her nipples.

"My apologies, maiden, but I cannot have you turning into a bull or a swan, or trying to run away," he said, in a voice slightly softer than before.

A bull? A swan? A strange suspicion started dancing through Helena's head. "Just what did you say your name was?" she asked him.

The man's chest swelled proudly, incidentally crushing her breasts beneath it. "I am Zeus, ruler of Olympus, seducer of maidens, wielder of the thunderbolt ... and you shall not escape me!"

"Why would I want to?" Helena practically cooed, as she laced her arms around his thick neck. That would explain how he got into her locked bedroom, the odd dream she'd been having ... it would explain a lot of things. She began rubbing her naked body against his, maneuvering so he could slide that gorgeous tool into the place where it belonged.

"Sorry?" he said. His voice suddenly seemed much less like massive thundering, and more like a pitiful squeak. He held his body very stiff as he stared down at her. While stiff was good in some ways, his stillness was somewhat of a problem now, as she couldn't get to quite the position she needed. "Are you not afraid of me? Will you not shift your form into a thousand others so as to escape? Will you not turn into a tree, a pebble, a breath of breeze?"

"Honey, I can't shift my form into even one other," Helena replied. She raked her nails along his back, and writhed her body underneath his, hoping to stimulate a response. His response wasn't quite what she expected.

"But it is simple. Even the shepherd maids of Greece knew how. Let me show you," he said. And with that, she felt an odd sort of twist in her brain, strange enough to make her pause a second in her feverish groping. Suddenly she knew how to change forms, how to become a thousand creatures of wind and flesh and earth. Zeus smiled in triumph above her. "Now, will you run?" he asked.

"Mmm ... I don't think so," Helena said. With that, she used her newfound knowledge to stretch her body, adding several inches to her height, and not so incidentally enabling her to finally slip that stiff penis inside her dripping cunt. Helena gasped then, and bit down on his rock-hard shoulder. She started to slide back and forth, almost gnawing on his skin as she did so.

138

"But they always run," Zeus said. He sounded dismayed. "I cannot believe women have changed so in the mere millennia that Hera and I spent traveling ... surely you are unnatural, a freak?"

Helena kept moving as she replied, "Well, my appetite's maybe a bit bigger than most women's, but I think I'm pretty typical nowadays." Suddenly, that feeling of delicious fullness started to disappear. Helena looked up in sudden suspicion. "Hey, if you're a god, surely you can keep it up?"

Zeus started to pull himself away. "You are a hellish imitation of a true woman. I will go and find a more feminine being in whom to spend my heavenly seed. You cannot expect me to perform with a creature as unwomanly as yourself. It would be ... unnatural!"

Helena suddenly clung even harder, wrapping her long (extremely long) legs around his muscular form. "Not so fast, boy. You look to be the best lay I've had in a long time." Helena's mind continued the sentence: *with potentially infinite endurance.* "You're not getting away until I get what you promised earlier. And not until I get it several times."

Zeus moaned in dismay, and suddenly changed himself into a porcupine. But Helena changed her skin into an odd fur, and stuck to him like Velcro. He wailed in horror, and changed himself into a lightning bolt. But she changed into a storm, and blew out all the windows as she surrounded him. Zeus moaned as he turned into a waterfall, pouring out of her forty-seventh-floor windows. But she turned into a river right below him, and engulfed his sweet essence. It was then that he really started to run.

Helena chased him down the highway, causing the early-morning traffic jams to become early-morning wrecking sites, as the heavenly dawn filled the sky. Irate businessmen in suits leaning out their car windows could hear a male voice, whimpering on the wind as the pair disappeared over the horizon. It was clearly calling, "Hera? Saaaaaaaave meeeeeeeee...!" The ones who listened carefully even heard a soft chuckle of what might have been goddess laughter as they hurriedly pulled their heads back inside, and quickly rolled up the windows.

Contributors' Notes

Gary Bowen has published over 100 short stories in anthologies and magazines and is the author of *Diary of a Vampire* (Masquerade Books, 1995), a finalist for the Bram Stoker Award in the category best first novel, and the collection *Man Hungry* (Masquerade, 1996). He can often be recognized at science fiction conventions on the East Coast by his white Stetson hat. He contributes regularly to Circlet Press erotic sf/f anthologies, and his work can be found in *Wired Hard*, *Wired Hard 2*, *Fetish Fantastic*, *Blood Kiss*, and other collections.

Kenneth Deigh lives, loves, and writes in the American Midwest. He is a healer and magickian with an interest in adapting eastern Tantric practices to western cultural milieu.

Jack Dickson: Fashion designer, linebacker, and iconoclast, Jack still finds time to explore worlds beyond the merely physical. A man of few words—specializing in those of four letters and under—he prefers to let his body of work speak for him. It's good to know someone's listening.

Raven Kaldera is a pansexual leatherpagan who practices sexmagick of various kinds. Raven edits the Scarlet Leather (the newsletter of NLA: New England) and has contributed stories to many Circlet Press anthologies, including *Blood Kiss*, *Erotica Vampirica*, *Genderflex*, *S/M Futures*, *Fetish Fantastic*, and others.

Robert Knippenberg: A 16-year-old trapped in a much older body, he writes obsessively, consumed by such questions as "How come aliens haven't abducted anybody kinky, who might really *like* all that stuff? Or is it that the only ones we see on TV are their *rejects*...?"

Albert J. Manachino has published over 100 short stories, but this is his first story to find a home with Circlet Press. He began writing to make his first granddaughter famous, eventually creating about thirty "Eugenia" adventures. He's fond of home-grown tomatoes, and this year, he and his wife, June, had to buy tomatoes only once.

Mary Anne Mohanraj is a writer of sf/f/h/erotica and poetry. Her erotic novella *Caught between Two Women* appeared in *Puritan* magazine, and an upcoming horror story, "A Dream of Wolves," will be in *Black October* magazine. Mary Anne is working on more material for *Puritan* and a more traditional fantasy novel set in a country much like India. She also moderates the Erotica Writers Workshop Online; feel free to e-mail her for details at moh2@midway.uchicago.edu, or visit her Web page at http://mud.bsd.uchicago.edu/~mohanraj/home.html.

Robert Rausch, cover photographer, started shooting his sister when she was sixteen years old. After he finished pre-med, he went to study photography in Paris. He worked as a photographer in Paris, New York, Los Angeles, Africa, and Atlanta. In 1991, he received a Master of Fine Arts degree at the Art Center College of Design. He works in Los Angeles now as an art director.

Thomas S. Roche has written fantasy and dark fantasy for such anthologies as *Gothic Ghosts, Northern Frights, Razor's*

Kiss, Enchanted Forests, and *The Shimmering Door.* His fiction and journalism on matters erotic have appeared in *Taste of Latex, Blue Blood, Black Sheets,* and *Boudoir Noir.* He is the editor of *Noirotica* (Masquerade Books, 1996) and co-editor of *Sons of Darkness* (Cleis Press, 1996). His work has appeared in numerous Circlet Press anthologies, including *Genderflex* and *Selling Venus.* He lives in San Francisco.

Cecilia Tan, editor, is the founder and publisher of Circlet Press. Her erotic short stories have appeared everywhere from *Penthouse* to *Ms.* magazine, and in anthologies like *Dark Angels, On a Bed of Rice, Best American Erotica 1996,* and *Best Lesbian Erotica 1997.* Her idea of magic is the transference of a concept from inside one person's head to another's—something sex, music, and short stories have been know to do, from time to time...

SexMagick
Women Conjuring Erotic Fantasy
Edited by Cecilia Tan

$7.95 • ISBN 1-885865-14-7

If you have enjoyed *SexMagick 2*, you may also enjoy the original volume of ritual magic, myth, and erotic power: *SexMagick*. A woman brings a jaguar idol to life and must overcome her repressions to appease the gods. An ancient fairy curse can be broken only with an erotic ritual. A musician cannot overcome his writer's block until he conjures a spirit from the past and communes with her. Includes the contributors Shariann Lewitt, Velma Bowen, and Reina Delacroix.

Circlet Press offers some of the most unique erotic literature being published today. We celebrate sex and sexuality through fiction that knows no boundary of imagination. Please ask for our titles at your local bookstore, or order them directly from us. To order within the U.S. and Canada, please send check or money order for the correct amount plus shipping and handling of $3 for the first book and $1 for each additional book. Please include a statement of your age and your complete return address. Overseas orders, please double the shipping amount.